AN IMPOSSIBLE LOVE

Elizabeth rose and attempted to leave. But the Lord of Giltham would not relinquish his hold on her and drew her to him instead, folding his arms about her and placing his face against her hair.

"You must know that I love you," he whispered. "You must."

The harder she struggled to free herself the more tightly he held onto her until she remained quiet. He felt her sobbing against his shoulder—quietly, softly, subdued. Until with a mighty effort, she freed herself and cried, "It cannot be. It cannot." She ran from the room and from the man she could never marry. . . .

THE SECRET OF GILTHAM HALL

by
Jeanne Cheyney

First Edition
July, 1980
ISBN 0-89191-326-2
LC 80-67636

Chapter 1

Elizabeth pulled the knocker on the servants' entrance of the great house of Giltham Hall and waited silently for whomever might chance to answer. The great imposing walls of the mansion frightened her. She'd overheard the villagers talk of the wild affairs that went on within these walls. The old master's recent death, they whispered, was caused by his extreme fondness for port.

But the summons was explicit. Elizabeth had no choice but to answer as bidden before the young Lord Giltham at ten o'clock this morning. But why did he want to see her? How did he even know she existed?

Norman, the footman, opened the door and peered out at her. "Yes, miss?"

"I am Elizabeth Bardwell, sir."

"Come in, Miss Bardwell. You are expected."

Elizabeth followed the middle-aged man down an enormous gray marbled passage, through great, carved oak doors into a library, and was told to be seated.

As she waited for the young master to appear she gazed at

the countless volumes of books resting neatly and well spaced on shelves that covered three walls of the mammoth room. Filtered sunlight streamed through a tall many-paned window, which held a cushioned windowseat.

Elizabeth was so delighted to see that many precious volumes collected in one room that she failed to hear the library door open and close softly behind her.

"What a wonderful way to spend a rainy afternoon," she said, thinking aloud.

"Yes, it is, Miss Bardwell. I've done it often." Jonathan Giltham smiled slightly at the startled girl and continued to walk slowly to the cherry desk in the center of the library.

Elizabeth colored and stood straight with her face to the window. She had only had a moment to glance at the young heir to Giltham Hall. His handsome countenance made her even more embarrassed to be caught talking to herself.

Jonathan suppressed his amusement and looked fixedly into her face while he motioned to the chair near the desk and placed his at such an angle that he could view the young woman at length and to best advantage.

"Be seated, Miss Bardwell, please."

Elizabeth seated herself in the armchair, placed her bonnet in her lap, and folded her hands in such a way as to keep the bonnet from falling to the floor.

For a few moments Jonathan studied her. She was even more beautiful than he remembered from seeing her at the Harvest Supper the night before. It was then that he had decided she would be his mother's new personal maid.

Even her clothes were handsomely made, showing to best advantage the lovely qualities of her well-developed body. The pale colors of the material enhanced her large blue eyes and shiny hair to perfection. For some strange reason she seemed entirely to belong to such a setting as this mansion.

When Elizabeth saw the master's fixed gaze upon her, she

looked down at her hands. But not before she noticed his strong but noble features. A strand of his blond hair fell over his forehead, making him look charmingly young.

"You are how old, Miss Bardwell?"

"Nineteen, my lord." She looked into his face to answer directly.

Jonathan nodded slightly and settled down more comfortably into his chair. "Tell me about yourself. Do you read?"

"Yes, sir."

"What, in particular?"

"The Scriptures, *Gulliver's Travels, Pilgrim's Progress, Paradise Regained.*"

"You are well read if you read them fluently. How did you get access to all these books?"

"They belong to my mother."

"And she reads them as well?"

"Yes, my lord."

"Isn't that rather unusual for a cottage woman?"

"I suppose it is."

Jonathan got up from his chair and walked over to a shelf from which he drew a small handsomely bound volume of one of the named books.

"Will you read a few passages for me, please?" After handing it to the girl, he once again seated himself in his chair, and waited to see what kind of performance she was capable of rendering.

Elizabeth immediately turned to a portion she loved,

"The brandisht Sword of God before them blaz'd
Fierce as a Comet; which with torrid heat,
and vapour as the Libyan Air adust,
Began to parch that temperate Clime——"

She read without flaw. So beautifully did she quote the chosen words that the master was moved, not only by the gentle tones of her voice but also by the deep feeling with which she read the passage. It would have pleased him to spend the whole morning listening. But, he must go on with the interview. There were other qualities he wanted to learn.

She handed him the volume and he rose to deposit it once more in its proper place on the shelf.

"What other accomplishments do you have?" The young man turned and walked back to his chair.

"I sew."

"Did you make the gown you are wearing?"

"Yes, my lord."

"Then you sew as well as you read. Tell me, did your mother teach you to sew?"

Elizabeth shook her head yes. "She is seamstress for your mother." She watched the young master rise from his chair and begin to pace about the room. She was beginning to feel somewhat like a poacher being questioned before a judge.

"You mentioned that you read the Scriptures, Miss Bardwell. Do you attend the Church of England regularly?"

"No, sir. I do not attend the village church."

The young master studied her carefully but she remained calm. "And where do you attend services. Are you Papist?"

"No, my lord."

"Where then?"

"Chapel, sir."

The man was silent as he reflected on her answer. So. Before him sat a Dissenter—a beautiful one at that. He was sure that the dingy interior of the chapel, whose austerity he had seen once out of curiosity, was greatly enhanced by this fair maiden. For a few moments he sat in meditation.

Then he leaned forward. "Miss Bardwell, we are joined to the Church of England, and therefore attend regularly, or rather, Lady Giltham attends regularly." Here he paused so as to think clearly through his words.

"I'm sorry to hear it, my lord."

"Sorry to hear what?"

"That you don't attend regularly."

"Yes, well, I am not as devout a Christian as my mother." Again he paused but Elizabeth remained silent.

"You understand, Miss Bardwell, that we require each member of our domestic staff to attend church with us. Lady Giltham will need someone beside her at all times for her comfort. You, of course, can understand that?"

"Yes, my lord. My faith is not dependent on a chapel room."

He truly hoped it was not, for he was by no means interested in losing the treasure seated before him. "Now, Miss Bardwell, you are capable of performing household tasks and knowledgeable in herbal remedies?"

"Yes, my lord."

Of the latter he was quite sure, for he had heard about the abilities of the dissenting women in making remedies. "And this you learned from your mother?"

She nodded her assent.

Jonathan now knew enough to convince him that this young woman was the one best suited for his mother's needs. Not only was she prudent and educated, but she was clever in answering his questions. If his mother had different opinions on the matter, he would see to it that she changed her mind.

He had one important question left before he would make his decision. He asked it last, to avoid appearing anxious. He stood up and faced the fireplace.

"Miss Bardwell, I will need to know if you are engaged to marry. You see, Lady Giltham will require a companion who is unmarried."

"A companion, my lord?"

"Yes, that's why I called for you."

Elizabeth stared at the young lord. He took much for

granted, and she would not have accepted willingly had it not been for the strangling rise in food costs and fear of enclosure, facing the villagers with poverty.

Elizabeth hesitated for a moment. "No, my lord, I'm not married," she finally whispered.

The answer pleased him more than he cared to admit. Nothing more remained to do, but to take Elizabeth to see Lady Giltham for final approval. He pulled the cord for the footman and left the room with a nod of his head. "Lady Giltham will see you shortly."

"Thank you, my lord."

Once again Elizabeth was left alone in the room for some time, and she began to study it carefully from where she sat. Heavy velvet draperies of a gold color hung in magnificent folds around the window, with this same gold color repeated in the carpeting and chairs. In the center of the side wall was an exquisitely carved chimney piece of marble, held up by angelic forms. Over it a mammoth gilt-edged mirror reached nearly to the base of the ceiling. For a moment she studied the wall by the fireplace. It seemed strange somehow.

Norman, the footman entered and led the way to the northern end of a huge passage. From there he made a right turn beyond an immense long clock and entered a smaller hall, made bright by a window facing out over the north garden. He held the door at the end of this hall open as he announced, "Miss Bardwell, my lady."

The room was a cheerful morning room of no large proportions with an adjoining bedroom to the side.

"Come and sit near me, Miss Bardwell." The lady motioned to a chair close by. She reclined on an elegantly embroidered satin daybed, upon which her silk skirts were arranged daintily.

The lady's face was stern. Indeed, many about her had often remarked that she had a look of granite, and many a gentleman, and lady as well, withered before her direct gaze.

"The master is well pleased with your abilities, Miss Bardwell. I will require much personal attention from you, and I expect that you will perform your duties well." Lady Giltham paused to make sure Elizabeth understood.

Then she continued. "You will occupy the small room next to mine—in there," she pointed to a small bedroom beyond the morning room, "so that I may command your services at all times. Your duties here will necessarily be performed in strict confidence and nothing of the family's personal business is to be repeated beyond these walls. Do you understand, Miss Bardwell?"

"Yes, my lady."

"I am told that you are a Methodist. This I find highly displeasing. There is no church as excellent as the Church of England in precepts and doctrines. You, of course, will attend with me, and you will perceive, I am sure, how base your beliefs are." Again the lady paused for the true worth of her words to penetrate fully.

Elizabeth remained calm and unmoved during the lecture, but anger kindled within her at the lady's blatant proclamations.

"Now, is your handwriting legible, Miss Bardwell? Do you have a good grammatical command of the English language?"

"Yes, my lady."

"Would you please take my pen and this sheet of writing paper and write the words I tell you?"

While Lady Giltham dictated the sentences, she watched the young woman write. Upon completion, she scrutinized the finished epistle with utmost care.

"You will do very well, Miss Bardwell—Elizabeth. At times it will be necessary for you to carry on my correspondence, since I am unable to write much of the time due to a stiffness of joints. Now I will have the footman show you to your room and a carriage will be sent for your things."

Lady Giltham raised her voice to rouse the footman who was standing just outside the door, and he led Elizabeth only a few paces to the door of a much smaller room, adjoining the ones occupied by Lady Giltham.

The room was comfortably furnished with a bed, night-stand, a wardrobe, and a stuffed chair pushed beneath the window.

After the footman left, Elizabeth went over to the window and looked out. From here she could assess each visitor who approached the main entrance to the house either by foot or on the causeway. The vastness of the house surprised her. It towered above her in symmetrical brickwork that skirted around the windows and melted into broad, vast chimneys. Elizabeth sighed. No one had even asked if she would accept the position. It was assumed that she would be honored to do so.

Chapter 2

During the next days, as Elizabeth went back and forth from the kitchen to fetch tea for Lady Giltham, she was amazed at the grandeur of the repasts prepared by Matilda Henneson, the cook. Elizabeth could not help thinking of the villagers, whose meager purses could no longer afford a bite of meat—except for an occasional hare that was poached at the peril of hanging or six months' imprisonment.

Elizabeth knew her father would say, "Obey them that rule over you." But it was a hard saying. Only softened by the thought of her father's face and the words she knew would follow, "If you have faith, God will provide."

Even though the villagers were not allowed to kill the animals that roamed the open land, the game warden soon told Jonathan that the woods were well stocked and could use a little thinning out. The young master sent invitations to four friends, including William Chesterton and Handly Hower, to join him for a week of hunting before the London season, now only four weeks away. And he invited the families of each to help ease Lady Giltham's pain at losing her husband.

He also invited the Sloanes—the family doctor, his wife, and daughter—to thank the doctor for his continuous care of Jonathan's father during his last days.

The guests arrived at four o'clock one afternoon in August with maids and valets, ready for a week of entertainment. Lady Giltham had felt a slight pain in her chest that morning, so she remained in her chambers with Elizabeth until it was time for dinner. Shortly before, she walked grandly down to the foyer, desirous of making a good impression, yet eager to play the part of the grieving widow.

She greeted the family friends and gladly accepted Dr. Sloane's escort into dinner. Once they were seated and had begun to eat the first course of their sumptuous meal, their conversation turned to enclosure, the wealthy landowners' attempt to add to their estates by fencing in open land and buying the lands of small farmers.

"Tell me, doctor," Lady Giltham said finally, "what do you think of enclosing the land?"

"You might do better, my lady, to ask what I think of bloodletting or leeches for aches and typhoid . . . But I must admit, I think enclosure can be a risky business. The initial expense is heavy."

"What expense could possibly be so heavy, doctor?"

"The costs of buying up the smaller farms, for one. Then there is the hedging and ditching, the manuring—and whatever else the land may require to be fertile enough for crops."

"Elias Shaftsbury, our new steward, favors enclosures," Lady Giltham stated decisively. "He says the yield in the end would be worth all this. Besides the dreadful war in America makes it necessary to have more food."

"Perhaps so." But the good doctor knew what lay within the inner regions of Lady Giltham's grand headdress and sharp features. The yield was not the major concern to her as much as the acquired social position of claiming the added acreage to the estate. The poor be hanged.

He began again to argue his point, using another approach. "The villagers and farmers will be forced to sell what little land they have, as well as lose their right to grazing a cow and sheep on the open fields. Or securing firewood from the common land. How will they live?"

"They would get wages for their work for us."

"Some things, my lady, are worth more than wages. Self-respect for one. When a man has owned a piece of land all his life, he feels of some worth to himself. Should this be denied him, he becomes a common laborer."

"It is in the making, doctor. It will come shortly. The request will go to Parliament when it convenes, won't it, Jonathan?"

The young lord shook his head without hearing what his mother referred to. Then he laughed at something Handly Hower told him and continued eating.

Knowing Lady Giltham could not be dissuaded, the doctor decided to change the subject. "So your friend Wesley has almost become respectable."

"That will never be," the lady hissed. "Never."

"He's got several magistrates' promises that he'll no longer be harassed."

"But he hasn't the church's permission to preach in its pulpits or ordain ministers, doctor. Nor will he ever."

"Who's to say. You must admit he's doing a lot of good. He's helped to calm the rioters in several parts of England. The same reports came from Scotland and Ireland."

"Hmph," said Lady Giltham. "Let's talk about something else. He's a disgusting little man."

The following morning when Lady Giltham arose she felt a slight pain down her arm. "Elizabeth, would you rub my arm. It seems a little numb."

"Shall I call Dr. Sloane?"

"No. Of course not. I probably laid on it and stopped the flow of blood." She leaned her head back and rested a moment.

"I'll have breakfast in the small dining room with the guests. Help me up."

Elizabeth accompanied the woman in to breakfast and helped her to her seat before she realized that three young gentlemen were already at table along with the ladies.

"I'm fine. Now go on to the kitchen and eat." Lady Giltham excused Elizabeth with a wave of her hand.

William Chesterton looked up from his plate and held his fork in midair as he stared at the girl moving quietly from the room out into the passage. "Jonathan, who is that girl?"

"Elizabeth Bardwell."

"When did you bring her here?" he whispered.

"A week ago."

"A maid?"

"Mother's waiting woman."

"I must meet her."

Handly Hower studied him with amusement and added, "She is a pretty little thing, I'll admit, if she knows enough English to carry on a decent conversation."

"I don't care in the least if she can or can't. I can talk for the both of us," William answered to dismiss Handly's objection.

The inclement weather that day forbade outdoor activity of any sort so the three young men left the table and retired to the billiard room for recreation. Soon William excused himself and made a path directly to the main passage to await the return of the Bardwell girl from the kitchen.

He hadn't long to wait. She came toward him while he stared out over the park from the nearest window, pretending not to notice her at all until she walked along directly behind where he stood. He turned suddenly and said, "Miss Bardwell?"

Elizabeth stopped and stared at the young man—shocked to hear her name coming from his lips. "Yes, my lord?" she said softly.

William looked into the face of the girl before him. Slowly he put out his hand to her as one would approach a deer—fearful lest it turn suddenly and dart away and the encounter be lost forever.

The girl continued to search his face for a few moments, unsure of his intentions. But when he said again softly, "Miss Bardwell," she raised her hand slowly. He grasped the small hand in his to bring it to his lips. He saw no flutter of her thick curling lashes in pretense of coquettish flattery, just a straightforward gaze of amazement that the young man would be so attentive to her a servant. She was not accustomed to such courtesies from anyone of the village. On the contrary she knew nothing but rebuke because of her religious beliefs.

William continued to study the girl for a moment longer. Then he said, "May I walk with you?"

Elizabeth looked down and turned. "If you wish, my lord." She proceeded to walk, keeping her eyes straight ahead.

"You've been here a short while, I'm told."

"One week."

"Will you accompany the family to London?"

"I can't say, my lord."

"Your father and mother live in the village?"

"Yes."

"What type of work is your father engaged in?"

"He is the village carpenter."

William found the girl's speech as genteel as the young ladies at the Hall, and he silently marveled at it. "Please excuse me for being inquisitive, Miss Bardwell, but you don't speak as most villagers. Have you been to school?"

"No, my lord."

"But how—?"

"My mother is solely responsible for my training." By this time Elizabeth had arrived at her door and put her hand to the latch, expecting to be excused.

"Please. Please, Miss Bardwell, walk to the end of the passage with me. Don't go just yet."

Elizabeth hesitated for a moment, and then looked up at the young man questioningly before she moved along with William toward the passage entrance some twenty feet away.

She neither shrunk from him nor was awed by him, but remained calm until she heard voices in the passage and turned. "I must go, my lord."

"Yes, I suppose you must but I've enjoyed talking with you, and I'll look for an opportunity to do so again." Then catching her hand, he pressed it to his lips before she glanced quickly into his face, nodded, and slipped away from him.

William waited until he heard the door latch before he turned and strolled back to the billiard room. He was well pleased with himself and more than ordinarily pleased with Miss Bardwell.

"Well, there you are," Handly called to the wanderer when he returned. "This oaf is beating me unmercifully and I need a rest. Take over for me."

Handly threw himself onto a couch, stretched full length, and folded his hands across his chest while Jonathan and William continued on with the game.

"How old is your Miss Bardwell, Jonathan?" William inquired.

"Nineteen."

"Are you still going on about that village wench?" asked

Handly. "Beware of a pretty face and no brains," he continued absently. "And no morals, whatever. They come easy. I know."

"I don't recall that I asked you." William studied his shot carefully.

"Hmph," said Handly. "You take girls like that but you don't marry them."

William watched for another opportunity to talk to Elizabeth and found that his diligence was rewarded the following afternoon when she slipped out a side entrance with a basket in hand and headed for the barns.

He waited until she was beyond the trees before he hurried to catch up with her. "Miss Bardwell, may I walk with you again?"

She glanced up suddenly and pulled her cloak closely about her. "If you like." The wind was chilling and the sun shown little through the cloud masses. Elizabeth half wished the plain young man would not accompany her but she said nothing.

"You enjoy walking?"

"Yes, my lord."

From a distance the hounds barked with unbounded enthusiasm, anxious to be after that elusive fox that so cleverly outsmarts men but gives them no less excitement.

"You do not enjoy hunting, my lord?"

"Not especially. It seems to me that it's a great amount of energy spent for a prize that is not likely to be won." He glanced at the girl beside him. "What are you gathering in your basket?"

"Apples from the barn."

They advanced a short while and William said, "Tell me, what interests you."

"Reading and languages—French in particular. Je parle courràment français, et j'aurais beaucoup de plaisir à vivre avec les gens de Paris," she answered.

"Ah! vous parlez bien le langage."

"My mother taught me."

"How is it that your mother was obviously a genteel girl, but married your father who is a carpenter. The social difference is obvious but not objectionable, of course."

"Love, my lord."

The wind increased to gusting, making further conversation impossible. Soon the two moved into the barn. When the basket was heaped as high as practicality allowed, they started back across the waste, glancing up to watch two riders approaching toward them from the woods.

"So there you are, William," said Handly. "We've searched everywhere for you."

"Whatever for?" he asked. "I'd hardly get lost around here."

Elizabeth moved on in silence, for she found it most embarrassing to be at some distance from the Hall with a guest of her employer. But since he had invited himself, she felt no guilt on her part whatever.

"You have a letter waiting for you, William. Your father sent us to locate you," Jonathan informed him.

"A letter? Ah! That could mean just one thing. Tell father I'm on my way."

"Want to hop on my horse?"

"No!" shouted William, running to catch up with Elizabeth and balancing the basket to avoid spilling the apples in the doing. "I've more interesting company and will get there eventually."

Jonathan studied the pair for a few moments, and then galloped after Handly.

Lord Chesterton waited in the gallery for his stepson's return. When at last the young man made his appearance, he motioned toward a seat and pulled a letter from his pocket.

William knew at once what it contained. "The commission, father?"

"Yes, William. It came through." He handed it to his stepson to read.

"It says that I am to report to London in one week. I'm grateful, father, for your efforts. I will take Samuel along with me."

"Of course." Lord Chesterton watched the boy depart and felt a thrill of pride, for he liked the boy as if he'd been his own. It had been that way since the first time he'd seen him at four years of age. When he fell in love with Lady Chesterton, she was a widow with two sons. He often regretted that he had named her older son his heir.

William had but four days left at Giltham Hall and determined to make the best use of it. He spent more and more time with the servant girl, accompanying her on errands, almost against her will. The first time he saw her he wanted her as his wife. After all, his fondest dream was to work one of his stepfather's estates and live in a house on the property. He wasn't interested in London society or the young women there who flitted from party to party.

The day before his departure William asked Jonathan to come to his chambers. William knew what his friend would say when he revealed his love for Elizabeth. But he owed Jonathan that much.

"Come sit by the fire, for it's a damp day and the heat feels good," he said as Jonathan entered.

"What have you in mind?" Jonathan asked, leaning his hands to the warmth of the flames.

"About Elizabeth—"

"Yes? What about her?"

"I am in love with her, and want your permission to ask her for her hand."

"It seems to me that her father would be the more likely one to speak to on such matters."

"I disagree. She is your responsibility, and I'll not let a

carpenter stand in the way of her being my wife."

"You know that she is a Methodist?"

"Yes."

"Have you asked her yet?"

"No. But I intend to."

"You should consider that you will be in the army," Jonathan reminded him. "America will be your battleground. You do not know when you will return or in what condition, for that matter. I suggest that you wait to propose marriage. Think of her, William, and what you ask."

"I have thought of all that and I mean to marry her."

"And she has told you she loves you?"

"I've not asked her to. Love, I am told, often follows after marriage—grows as a plant."

"I still say, wait," Jonathan said, his voice rising slightly.

"And I cannot accept it. She's all I think about. If my commission had been refused, I would marry her now and make my living as a farmer."

"If you are so set on this scheme, why do you even bother to ask me for my permission?"

"As a courtesy."

Jonathan sighed. *Why should I care,* he thought. *She is nothing to me.*

The following morning Dr. Sloane and the Chestertons left the manor—the doctor heading for London and the Chestertons to their home to make preparations for William's forthcoming departure.

Jonathan bid William good-bye, but he didn't ask about Elizabeth. Whatever was decided was best left unsaid. Who could say what might happen before William came back to claim the girl for his own.

Chapter 3

By late afternoon of the next day two more of Jonathan's friends, Samuel Pickens and Edward Finnius, arrived for hunting before they continued on to their London lodgings and Parliament.

While the young lost sight of time in light prattle and amusement, Lady Giltham endeavored to dismiss her continual tiredness and the recurrent pain in her chest. Her show of lightheartedness affected the older women, Lady Hower and Lady Sloane, making them feel that they truly did her good with their presence.

Once I get to London I shall feel better, Lady Giltham reasoned. *It's the gloom of the weather that depresses me. I could never tolerate a winter here alone.* She kept up the smiles and the gracious chatter until supper that evening ended and the hour was such that she could withdraw without causing suspicion.

Elizabeth ate her supper with the servants, and then retired with a candle and a novel William had gotten for her in Dumford the day before.

She sighed and thought about the past week. William's profession of love and marriage had left her breathless, but not entirely in love as she always thought love should be. William was very plain, although the uniform of the regiment might remedy that.

Then she thought of Jonathan—tall, handsome, fair-haired Jonathan. But as a penniless servant she had little choice. William, too, would have little as the second in line to inherit Chesterton Manor.

When Lady Giltham called, Elizabeth rose, helped her undress, and put her to bed.

"Can I call for a doctor, my lady? You look tired and not well."

"All I need is rest," snapped Lady Giltham. "I'll be fine tomorrow. Go back to your reading. I don't want to be disturbed."

"Yes, my lady." For some time Elizabeth read, and then she wandered to the passage window, looked out over the moon-bathed lawns to the groves of motionless trees beyond, and wondered what her father and mother were doing at this hour. Her eyes stared in blank reverie, when she noticed a movement along the carriage path and became alert to the advancing steps of a small boy and a huge dog toward the rear of the house.

What could a child be doing out at such an hour of the night? she wondered. *And what business could he possibly have at the house?* Elizabeth studied the situation for a few moments before the boy disappeared behind the manor. Her curiosity was piqued so she stood trying to reach a reasonable conclusion until the child reappeared and hurried at a much greater pace back along the path from which he had emerged. Elizabeth watched until he disappeared from sight, and then she turned, slightly chilled from standing in the cold passage, and walked back to her warm hearth.

For some time she read and became absorbed in the

novel. Then a knock sounded lightly on her door. She jumped slightly, for she was startled at the suddenness of the intrusion into her solitude.

"Miss," the valet said, "the master requests your presence in the drawing room."

Elizabeth frowned at the summons and turned to brush her hair and change into a fresh gown. *What could the directive mean?* she wondered.

But she walked up as bidden and entered quietly into the huge well-lit room, where the master and his guests were busily engaged in cards and boisterous conversation. For a few moments she remained at the door, closing it softly behind her and glancing at young Lord Giltham.

The bottles of port were distributed about the room; glasses were filled and refilled. Elizabeth sat on a chair nearest the door until Handly spotted her and called out in slurred speech.

"Ah, Miss Bardwell, come. We have a request of you."

Elizabeth rose and crossed the room while the young men silently stared at the pretty girl.

"Can Lady Giltham spare you for a while?" Jonathan asked.

"She is sleeping, my lord."

"Excellent. We need another partner as we're shy one young lady for pairs. But before we begin charades, will you play and sing for us? There is a guitar in the corner."

The room grew suddenly silent; every eye focused on the girl standing before them.

Elizabeth was stunned. She glanced about the room at the occupants—some very unsteady on their feet—and she felt a revulsion in their presence. She regretted ever telling Jonathan that she played the harp and guitar and sang a little.

Jonathan put his glass to his lips and watched her above the rim to see what she would do. She turned to him, lifted her eyes squarely to his, and said softly, "I doubt that you or your guests would find my song pleasing."

"Nonsense. We'll be the judge of that. Come. Get the guitar and favor us with a number or two."

Elizabeth nodded her head slightly and did as she was bidden. The instrument was standing in the corner and quite out of tune, so she tightened some of the strings, loosened others to the required pitch, and then proceeded to strum softly in preparation for her song.

At an earlier time of day the genteel group before her might have caused her to panic. But in the present state—the near drunkenness, the silly giggling flirtatiousness of the girls—she neither feared them, nor wished to remain in their presence at all.

The candlelight threw a soft glow on her pretty face—added gleam and lustre to her raven locks and the folds of her plain gown—but did not detract from her blue eyes. While the young men stared in rapt attention at her simple beauty, the young ladies arched their brows and threw back their heads at the servant who dared come into their presence and draw all eyes from them.

Elizabeth looked down at the instrument in her hands and formed the words.

"My mind to me a kingdom is,
Such present joys therein I find
That it excels all other bliss
That earth affords or grows by kind—"

The room was wrapped in silence as the girl completed the verses of her song. Her voice was not special, but it was soft and sweet.

When yet another song was requested, she simply shook her head, set the guitar aside, and would have slipped from the room. But Handly, who by this time was loud and boisterous from drink, called to Elizabeth for a kiss.

She looked about for Lord Giltham. *Surely he won't per-*

mit this behavior toward me. But he was not in the room. Before she could leave, the young men gathered about her. Handly waved his glass and approached her.

"Come, give Handly a nice kiss, Miss Bardwell." He put his liquored breath close to her nostrils.

"No," said Elizabeth. "I shall not."

The other young women saw that she was cornered, but refused any assistance. They carefully watched the foolish antics of the young men.

When Elizabeth adamantly refused Handly's offer, Betsy Hower called out angrily, "Do you really want a kiss from an orphan? Ha! Such a prize! Such filth!"

Elizabeth hadn't realized that these young women knew anything about her background. Did they know that Matthew Bardwell, the only father she knew, had found her hidden in the old master's coach one day as he was returning from an errand in Linton? When no one claimed her, the Bardwells, who were childless, had raised her as their own.

"So you're an orphan wench, eh?" Handly laughed and moved in closer.

Elizabeth attempted to slip by him before he grabbed her, but it was useless. He sat down on a chair and turned her roughly over his knee; then he lifted her skirt and smacked her hard on her seat.

Elizabeth wrenched loose of the drunken man, tore from the room, and fled to the back staircase. Soon she was in her room, tears of anger welling up in her eyes.

Eerie, ghostlike shadows danced across Elizabeth's room like giant, swaying monsters of another world. She shuddered and moved noiselessly. The stone floor was chilling. After throwing a blanket around her shivering body, she knelt and tried to stir new life into a dusty gray log that had burnt crimson and hot just hours before. But life was not there. It lay ashen, still and dead.

Elizabeth climbed into bed and pulled the blankets tightly around her neck to rid herself of the sudden chill of the cold floor. From the dark misty beyond came her recollections of the disgusting scene in the drawing room. Her body twisted in sudden torment as she remembered it all again and the heat of her anger drove the chill from her body as a scythe severs the heady grains from the stalk.

Elizabeth put her hands to her face—covering eyes that spilled forth hot tears. From every limb she shook with penned-up emotion. "I must walk. Anywhere. Just walk."

She knew every step of the passage, what to avoid bumping into in the dark, where to turn. It was black as a vault, except for the faint shafts of pale light that came treading in weirdly grotesque shapes across from the library window.

How long she walked along the passage she neither cared nor comprehended. The passage clock struck the hour of three as she leaned weary and spent against the cold passage wall.

When she finally pulled her chilled body away and moved silently back to her chamber and into bed, sleep came immediately.

She hated facing the servants the next day. But hunger finally caused her to creep quietly out into the passage and make her way to the kitchen.

She opened the door and was thankful for the bustling sounds of the pans and spoons. The servants were seated at the big table eating their bread and tea when she slipped into her place as inconspicuously as she could.

Norman, the footman, noticed her first. "Well, here's our singer! You really were a hit last night, eh, Elizabeth?" He laughed loudly and hit his hand on the table.

"How did it feel to sing for real gentlemen?" asked Nancy, the kitchen maid, with a glint of romance in her eye. "I'd be happy to."

"If ye asks me, it's wot ye deserve, Miss Bardwell. Talkin' like the rich ladies, and bein' nothin more 'n a servin' maid," said Matilda Henneson, testing the oven with a straw. "Hand me those loaves, Nancy, and be quick about it. The oven's just right."

Elizabeth sighed and drank her tea. She wanted to be allowed solitude, but she knew, also, that the incident had to be talked about before it would be dismissed.

"I played because I was bidden," she said calmly.

Nancy smiled a tiny smile of admiration for her fellow servant. "It took a bit 'o tartar, eh, Elizabeth?"

"A bit, yes," was her answer, stuffing the last bit of bread into her mouth and pushing away from the table.

She walked quickly from the room as the bell sounded from the lady's chamber.

Elizabeth longed to go out into the fields and run and cry to get rid of her melancholy. If only she could talk to her father. He always had words of wisdom to soothe her wounds. But she rarely had free time to visit her parents. She was alone and forsaken in the ancient mansion.

When Elizabeth returned to Lady Giltham's room, she sensed a tension in the lady's face. "I will go in to breakfast in a moment, but I'll take my toilet case now."

Elizabeth nodded and proceeded to help Lady Giltham dress.

"It's such a dreadful day I will just sit in the drawing room with Lady Sloane. See what you can do about my hair. It's a fright." She looked unhappily into her mirror and scowled while Elizabeth combed with as much gentleness as she could.

Elizabeth said nothing about the night before, choosing to forget the matter as best she could. "While you visit I would like permission to go to the woods, for there is a flower there that is an excellent remedy. Perhaps it would benefit you."

"Flower, indeed. What I need is a change of scenery—a transporting to London. Then I shall feel better. However, if you are bent on it, go."

"Thank you, madam."

As soon as she had taken Lady Giltham into breakfast with Lady Sloane, Elizabeth put her cloak around her, took up the basket, and started off, unaware of being followed.

From the house she followed the pathway that led into the woods. The groves were windswept and fresh bathed from the past days of rain. The thorn hedges already were drifting into scarlet adornment and the bittersweet bore glorious autumn coloring. Even the elms displayed a few bright patches of burnt gold amidst their greenery as if to hold onto the summer finery as long as they dared.

The wind whipped the grasses into a nodding frenzy and each tree trembled in humble submission. *Even the trees are made to obey the discipline of the elements,* Elizabeth thought.

She pulled her cloak closer about her as the wind played daring games with her skirts and dancing curls. It all added vigor to her aching chilled limbs, and she felt suddenly released from servility into such a delirious freedom that she wanted to sing and cry to the gathering clouds. The density of the woods engulfed her, and she looked up in admiration at the profusion of beauty surrounding her. Each trunk, leaf, and delicate stem was a crowning glory of the Creator's handiwork.

The light was fading rapidly, and Elizabeth scanned the overhead foliage for a patch of sky and signs of rain. With haste she gathered her blooms and darted quickly back to the semiclearing. The clouds began to pour forth their weepy liquid, and here and there drops found their way to the moist floor of the woods.

At the clearing she stopped for an instant, deciding whether to flee back into the density of the woods or seek cover beyond the clearing. As the rain pelted to the earth in dull thuds, she pulled her cape about her head and dashed wildly across the clearing toward an old hut, disappearing inside.

Elizabeth leaned against the door and closed her eyes. Her head pounded with pain and her cheeks burned. She was beginning to realize that the flush she had felt the night before came from more than just embarrassment. She shook her cloak to remove the moisture before it seeped into the fibers and made it damp throughout. She was chilled and went to the fire to stir the dying embers into a breath of life and heat. The girl leaned down and gently blew until a tiny spark leaped into a glowing ember before she scooped up some dry chips and fed them into the hungry little ember, causing it to leap into a flame.

From the floor Elizabeth pulled a dry log into the flames and coaxed the fire to take hold. The fire felt warm and soothing while the rain pelted and stung the small window nearby. She pulled the little stool to her and rubbed her shoulders for heat. The sound of the pelting rain and thunder filled the cottage.

Suddenly Elizabeth felt warm hands on her shoulders. She froze in terror before turning and staring into the face of the Lord Giltham who looked into her eyes and held her firmly.

Elizabeth uttered a startled cry and drew back with great force. The terror of the past night flashed before her in an instant, and she struggled to free herself from his grasp. His grip on her arms tightened. When he drew close and placed his warm lips on hers, she wrenched loose from him. Grabbing her cloak, she dashed wildly out into the storm, across the clearing, and back into the woods beyond.

"Come back!" he shouted. "You'll come down with a deathly fever!"

But she was gone. Her basket lay where she had placed it beside the banging door.

Jonathan made his way with haste to his horse and raced wildly onto the clearing. Then he searched the woods for a glimpse of the girl. Soon Jonathan spotted her, sprawled on the wet ground beneath a huge oak. She was breathing but unconscious.

Jonathan jumped from his horse and picked up her limp rain-soaked body. He placed her across the sodden beast's neck before he leaped up behind her and rode back toward the cottage. The rain resumed and was now a steady drizzle as they rode into the lean-to beside the hut. Jonathan placed her once again over the horse's neck and dismounted with great care. Then he carried her back into the small cottage.

The Lord Giltham was unaware of the bleating of sheep, and when he entered the hut was stunned to find a shepherd, who apparently inhabited the crude dwelling, rising to meet him.

The shepherd gasped when he saw Elizabeth. "What happened to her?"

"Just help me, will you?"

The shepherd motioned toward his bed, and Jonathan laid her carefully on the simple construction.

"Got any blankets? We'll have to get her out of these wet clothes."

The shepherd scurried to a rack and returned with two tattered blankets.

Jonathan ran the back of his hand across his mouth. "If you'll cover her with the blanket, I'll get the wet clothes off."

The shepherd obeyed and put the blanket over Elizabeth while Jonathan pulled the soggy garments from her body.

"Now wrap her tightly, shepherd. And get another blanket."

The old man brought a heavy wool mantel and proceeded to tuck it about her when he noticed the lump on her head. "How did she get a nasty knob like that?" he asked.

"She fell," was all the explanation Jonathan felt compelled to give. "Got any brandy?"

"A little."

"Get it."

Jonathan put his arm under Elizabeth's neck and drew her up slightly. The blanket slipped down to reveal her shoulder, slender and white, and her head fell against his arm with the damp hair matted to the wound on her forehead. He gently pulled the enmeshing strands back from her burning face before he took the bottle and glanced at the contents. "You were right when you said you had a little. Is this all?"

"Yes, my lord."

"All right, now, help me," Jonathan directed curtly.

The shepherd moved Elizabeth's lips apart gently, and the liquid rolled into her mouth. At the sting of the liquid Elizabeth moved slightly in Lord Giltham's arms and choked. Jonathan jerked her up and she moaned. For a moment her head pulled away from Jonathan's shoulder and then fell. The men watched and waited.

"Poke the fire and get it warmer in here, shepherd." When he placed his hand on her forehead and let it slide gently down her face, Jonathan realized that she was burning with fever—giving a glazed, pink color to her skin. A trembling to her body warned of chills throughout her entire frame.

Jonathan bit his lip and wondered what he was to do about the girl. She couldn't be moved and he couldn't leave her here alone with the shepherd. He stared down at Elizabeth, studied the flattering disarray of her black curls about her face and neck. Had it not been for the shepherd, he would have bent down and kissed the fair cheek until she regained full consciousness once again and looked up into his face. While he continued to stare she opened her eyes. The lids slid closed again and then parted with a startled gaze in finding Lord Giltham holding her in his arms. The full impact relayed throughout her entire body, and she cried out weakly, "No! Let me go."

"Hush. It's all right," he whispered softly. "You had a fall, but you're fine now. You will need to rest."

Elizabeth stared about the room without comprehending where she lay. When she moved her arms under the blanket and realized that she was undressed, she drew her hands to her flushed face and tried desperately to draw herself away from the master. She had just worked her hands free and pulled the blanket around her neck when the convulsive shivering began once again.

"Perhaps some herb tea, my lord?" the old shepherd offered, showing an obvious concern for the girl.

"Fix it," Jonathan ordered as he released his hold of Elizabeth and covered her carefully.

Jonathan picked up her clothes and hung them on a rope above the hearth to dry; then he walked to the tiny window to peer out. The rain had ceased and no sound but the bleating of the sheep could be heard from the outside. He ambled out to the lean-to, patted his horse, and moved beyond the shelter to study the sky overhead.

Above a grove of low trees the chimneys of Giltham Hall were barely visible. He knew he'd have to return to the house and give account to his mother for Elizabeth's extended absence from her side. Besides the girl obviously needed medical care so he would have to fetch an apothecary. The best thing to do was to leave now and return later with the apothecary and a maid to spend the night in the cottage with Elizabeth. There was little possibility that the girl could be moved in her present condition. Jonathan went back inside to check Elizabeth again and tell the shepherd of his decision; then he rode swiftly across the clearing toward the park and Giltham Hall.

It was an hour before Jonathan returned with the apothecary and Nancy, the kitchen maid. The shepherd was giving Elizabeth more liquid when the three came into the room.

While the apothecary mixed a potion for the girl, Jonathan asked the shepherd to help him bring in straw to make a bed for Nancy. "She'll stay with Elizabeth tonight and by tomorrow perhaps I can take her back to the Hall."

The shepherd moved silently toward the small stack of hay in the yard and proceeded to help the master until there were two beds, comfortable and waiting, upon which Jonathan placed blankets.

Soon the apothecary packed his few pieces of equipment and returned to his horse, but Jonathan stayed behind long enough to check the girl's fever once more. Then he looked about the room and said, "Take good care of her and I'll return in the morning."

"Yes, me lord," said Nancy, curtsying and looking shyly about at the room and the shepherd. She wasn't overly excited about staying in the hut, but she was happy, more than willing, to do it for Elizabeth.

After the men left and the shepherd went out to check his sheep, Nancy helped Elizabeth into the heavy linen gown Nancy had brought for her. Throughout the night she administered the medicine the apothecary had left, cooled Elizabeth's burning face with a moistened cloth, and gave her sips of herb tea. By morning the fever had abated, and Nancy was sure Elizabeth could be moved.

When the shepherd went to tend his flock at sunrise, Nancy began to dress Elizabeth. But she was so weak that it took a long time to get her clothes on her body. When the ordeal was completed, Elizabeth lay back on the simple bed, exhaused and ready to sleep once more.

At nine o'clock Lord Giltham rode up to the hut. He

called before he entered, and when Nancy gave him permission, he came into the room and walked directly to where Elizabeth lay.

"How are you feeling this morning, Elizabeth?" he asked softly.

"Better, thank you, but I'm so tired."

Jonathan knelt, balancing on his toes and leaning one arm over a knee, and studied her face.

She opened her eyes and saw the handsome and fair-haired Lord Giltham run his fingers slowly over his upper lip, studying her intently.

The fire burned brightly and the flames leapt in the air, the brilliance reflecting in the girl's flushed eyes. Jonathan could do nothing but stare at the simple beauty lying exhausted and spent. He reached over and placed his hand on her forehead. The fever was down, that was certain enough.

Suddenly he arose and faced Nancy. "You may leave and go back to the Hall."

"Yes, me lord," said the girl quietly; curtsying in a flustered manner before the gentleman. In an instant she was out the door and on her way across the woods.

Jonathan turned and glanced down at Elizabeth. She uttered no words, simply lay on her side and stared into the fire as if he didn't exist at all.

"I shall carry you to my horse and take you back to the Hall," he whispered at last. Then lifting a blanket he added, "We'll wrap you in this for the air's cold. I'll come for the remaining ones later."

Elizabeth tried to rise but felt unsteady and nauseous with the sudden effort. She put her hand to her eyes for a moment to settle her whirling faculties. Then Lord Giltham placed the wrap lightly about her shoulders and lifted her in the air to transport her to the waiting beast outside in the lean-to. Jonathan jumped up behind her, arranged the drapery against the chill, and urged the horse on.

Elizabeth tried to sit upright but could in no wise do so, for she grew nauseous once more; she placed her hand over her face to control the reaction in her stomach. Jonathan pulled her against his shoulder. She was too weak and sick to voice objection though he felt her push away from him in an effort to right herself and maintain her balance.

The air ripped at her blanket but Jonathan kept it secure. When they entered the woods, he looked down at the girl leaning against him and spoke. "I'm truly sorry, Elizabeth, about the episode with Handly in the drawing room. I was told, of course—much later."

Elizabeth made no comment. All she wanted was her own warm bed.

Chapter 4

Elizabeth remained in bed for two days, recovering from the fever and ague. Nancy felt that Elizabeth was her sole responsibility and fussed over her as a hen over a brood, feeling honored to be asked to see that she regained her proper health.

Jonathan talked with his mother frequently and laid out plans for departure to London in about two weeks. Lady Giltham felt much improved and her spirits rose, for she'd leave for London soon and enter society with a fresh vigor in spite of her black widow's gowns.

The ladies met after breakfast in the drawing room, seated about the fire.

"Adelaide, Jonathan's health appears excellent. His recent tour matured him and has seemed to give him a brighter outlook. He's so handsome! What a prize he will be for the right young lady!" said Emily Sloane. "Will he sit for Giltham in Parliament?"

"Yes, those are his exact plans. But we are mainly concerned with improving the estate—getting enclosure under way."

"Ours is completed now," said Mary Hower. "And with the increase in rents we are making handsome profits, I must confess. Actually doubled our income! With the markets in London in such great demand, we've a ready buyer for all we produce—especially the soft fruits and corn."

Lady Chesterton threaded a needle and began to sew on a sampler as she talked. "With the added land you can do so much to improve the estate—plant groves, make winding walkways and fish ponds, and drain marshes to reclaim more land."

"We certainly intend to do it all," said Lady Adelaide Giltham. "Our new steward, Elias Shaftsbury, recently posted a notice on the door of the church, warning the villagers of enclosure."

"Strange one, your Shaftsbury," Lady Sloane commented. "What made Lord Giltham hire him?"

"Pity for what happened to his family, I suppose. And he needed a man with a good business head. My husband never cared much for running the estate. When our old steward died, Elias seemed just the person."

"Whatever caused old Lord Shaftsbury to do away with himself?" Lady Hower asked as she took another stitch in her sampler. "Surely gambling debts would not have done it. He could have raised his tenants' rents and made his debts good eventually."

"Not so, I'm told. He played for the estate and lost. Hazard was the game, I believe. Strange thing, though, one thousand pounds have never been accounted for. The two sons were left penniless, you know, although Elias mentioned he hopes to purchase it back one day. The new owner does nothing with the property but let it go to ruin."

"So I hear," said Lady Hower. "What does Elias's brother do?"

"Proprietor of the White Hart Inn in the village. He's in charge of the poor law for the district and a good churchman. Quite devoted—Elias and his brother, James. They spend much time together."

"By the way, Adelaide, where is your waiting maid?" asked Lady Sloane.

"She's got the ague from a sojourn in the damp woods."

None of the ladies referred to the spanking incident—the sufficient humbling that the young men incurred on the brazen little thing who had the audacity to show her face in the drawing room and make a fool of herself.

Jonathan slipped into Elizabeth's room frequently to inquire about her health, for his conscience bothered him somewhat and he did feel responsible for the accident.

The young man would sit by Elizabeth or stand and gaze silently down into the sleeping face of the girl, whose raven hair, spread in loose array about her face, caused a quickening of his pulse. At times he had the almost uncontrollable urge to bend down and enfold her in his arms, but he knew from experience that she would permit none of it. There was a genuine purity about the girl that made him realize he'd do nothing to sully that virtue.

At times Elizabeth would awaken and find Lord Giltham sitting by her bed—or standing and looking down at her—and she grew uneasy. She must make every effort to be up and about. But she was weak and her efforts were of no avail.

By the end of the week Lady Giltham and Jonathan bid farewell to their guests and began serious plans for their departure to London. They met with their new steward to discuss his plans for the winter months.

Elias would remain at the house and oversee the estate.

"Lose no time, my lord, in getting the enclosure bill passed, before the villagers claim their rights to farm strips of the open land during the coming year," Elias warned Jonathan. Then he excused himself to attend to some personal business.

"We can be thankful we're leaving the estate in such able hands, Jonathan," said Lady Giltham. "Pay close heed to his advice for he is a prudent man and you will profit by his wisdom."

"But the man didn't need to post the notice until the enclosure bill was signed."

"Of course he did. Men need to be told of coming events. Let's say it was a courtesy to the villagers, shall we?"

Jonathan wasn't convinced and he couldn't quite say why he even cared. He never gave a thought to it before.

There were mixed feelings when the servants found out that Elias would remain at the Hall, for there would be no relaxing of minds or hands with him about, they were sure.

Elizabeth was told by Jonathan that she would accompany them to London. For her, it may as well have been the faraway land of America for she could not imagine what city living would be like with no woods or meadows, no feeling of open space, to relax in. The stories of smoke and filth did little to relieve her mind. Yet it held some fascination for her as a new experience. And she'd heard of the great meetings with Mr. Wesley at the Foundry there. She was determined to see the chapel firsthand and attend whenever she found him preaching within the city.

Elizabeth longed for true Christian fellowship. She had seen little of her own family since she came to the great house, and had not even been able to attend the chapel. She hungered for the blessing of inspired words that would edify and encourage her heart. And for the love of fellow believers to support her when she felt lonely and discouraged.

Five days before departure Elizabeth was preparing Lady Giltham's gowns for packing when she heard the woman fall—gasp for breath and clutch her chest. The girl rushed to her mistress, searched her face, and then ran out into the passage to find Lord Giltham as quickly as possible. After running the full length of the passage, she found a servant who knew his whereabouts and went to fetch him.

Jonathan ran to his mother's chambers, followed closely by the valet, and found Elizabeth kneeling by her on the floor, trying to make her as comfortable as possible under the circumstances. The men lifted the woman gently from the cold floor and placed her on her bed.

She continued to gasp for breath.

Jonathan turned to his valet and ordered, "Get to Dumford with all speed and fetch the doctor; then send a message by late coach to London for Dr. Sloane. Get Elias to write the letter. Now hurry!"

"Yes, m' lord."

Elizabeth placed a cool cloth on the lady's forehead and hurried to get another blanket from the chest to keep her warm.

Jonathan paced the floor and sat by his mother's bed in intervals. The sudden illness was a blow. Absolutely. He could see his well-laid plans disintegrate and crumble as so much powder at his feet.

He watched Elizabeth care for his mother—her slender body leaning over her, her fingers moving surely—and he had a feeling of despair at the thought of leaving her behind. The trip after a heart attack, and he was sure it was just that from the symptoms he'd witnessed, was no longer a possibility. He had looked forward to having Elizabeth with him in London: to look for when he arrived back at the house—to go walking and riding with and to talk to. He ran his fingers through his light hair.

When Dr. Sloane arrived from London at sundown the next night, he verified the diagnosis as a heart attack, ordering complete bed rest and little exertion.

Elizabeth attended her mistress night and day, disregarding her own weariness until the doctor finally insisted that she go for a walk in the air while he kept a vigilant watch.

Elizabeth slipped her cloak around her shoulders and strolled across the park until she came upon a rise above the fields. The aromas of wheat and barley still clung to the harvested strips even in their sheared bareness, and the cows were eagerly foraging to satiate their perpetual hunger and add flesh to their meager frames. She stood transfixed and filled with unbelief that strips of the open land would no longer exist as each man's share of ancient dignity and independence. The cows, a symbol of sufficiency and pride, might never again be seen on the common waste. The injustice of it filled her with anger and deep sorrow on behalf of a proud but simple people.

The day grew overcast, gloomy and foreboding, and smelled of rain. From across the barren strips the wind no longer was held in check by the seas of grain but whipped at her cloak.

A lone horseman sauntered to a standstill beside the girl's straight figure and remained silent for some minutes until Elizabeth moved her head slowly to one side. Her eyes settled first on the horse and then on the rider himself. She gazed momentarily into his face. "My lord," she whispered and turned her face back again toward the fields.

"The air smells of rain," he said.

"Yes, it does." They both continued to gaze across the fields until Lord Giltham swung his foot back over his horse and dropped to the ground. With slow, deliberate paces he walked to the rise, put his hands on his hips, and then turned to the girl beside him.

"It must be done, you know, Elizabeth." He spoke softly.

"Does it, my lord?"

He dropped to his knees, pushed his hat foreward on his head, and sat with his torso leaning forward and his fore-arms resting on his knees. "I'm afraid so." He motioned to the ground beside him. "Come and rest."

"And at so great cost, my lord?" She refused to be seated, for by now she had to bridle her rising anger. "Have you ever felt hunger? A grinding uncontrollable hunger? And heard the pitiful cries of a child who in his lack of understanding pleads for a morsel of crust when there is none to give?"

Her breast heaved as she continued and her voice gained passion. "How, my lord, do you explain to a child that he has no milk because there is no longer a cow. Or that he has no bread because there is no longer wheat to be ground?"

"Come, Elizabeth, it's not as bad as the picture you paint." He leaned back on one arm and bent a knee upward. "Other areas have enclosed their lands with great success and had surplus to sell in the markets of London, benefiting not only the landowner but also the villagers."

"The benefit, I fear, is not equally shared, my lord. For the pain from one quite outweighs the satisfaction from the other."

"It doesn't have to be as you describe, if planned with care."

"True. It does not have to be. But it is. And who cares? Is it not true that the wealthy become wealthier?"

"I cannot deny it."

"And the wealth that is reaped, is it again shared with the poor of the land at whose expense it was secured? I fear not."

By now Lord Giltham enjoyed the fiery eloquence pouring forth from this girl, and he lay back and smiled. "You're beautiful when you're angry," he teased.

She bit her lip and stared over the fields. Hot tears filled her eyes but were dried by the gusts that bathed her face, for she was too distraught to answer such folly.

A few droplets of water plummeted from the overcast sky and fell on Lord Giltham's cheek. He arose quickly.

"Come," he said. "Let's return before we're drenched."

Elizabeth turned and together they raced to the park, pulling the horse behind. They found a measure of shelter beneath the partially barren trees as they pushed on toward the manor beyond.

By the time the two reached the clearing at the edge of the park, the rain descended in a steady drizzle and played a staccato tune on the dry leaves overhead.

Lord Giltham studied the girl beside him, for the running enhanced the color of her cheeks and lips and the rain added a sensuous moisture that drew his emotions forward once more. He knew the two of them were well hidden from prying eyes, and he longed to fling his arms about her and draw her to him. But as he put his hand toward her she escaped across the clearing to the stables and disappeared within.

The rain now fell in torrents, and he was stranded beneath the overhang with little hope of escaping his prison of oaks for some time. He leaned back against a huge tree to avoid erratic showerings of droplets from various directions and drew his coat about his throat. His mind was filled with Elizabeth and her effect on him. She whetted his appetite to ravenous hunger by her elusiveness. He doubted that a malicious trait could be found within her, but she was such a thing of mystery to him. Whatever her game, he indeed had plenty of time and could wait—if it were not for William.

When a lull in the deluge presented an opportunity for escape, he jumped onto the horse's back and raced to the shelter of the stables. The groom rushed to aid Lord Giltham with his horse and motioned toward the saddle room.

"We've a fire going, m' lord. If ye don't mind, it would take the chill out 'o ye." The master swung down from his horse and wandered into the adjoining room where a blazing fire was dancing on the hearth. In a corner on a stool

Elizabeth sat huddled with her chin resting on her clasped hands.

"Sit here, close to the fire," she said, and knelt on the hearthstone so he could move in.

"So," he whispered, raising his eyebrows and tilting his head. "I detect a note of warmth in those icy veins, Miss Bardwell."

Elizabeth rose from the hearth and put her hands to the heat. "A fire feels good, doesn't it, my lord." She still faced the grate and did not look at him.

"Yes," he answered briefly, willing to let her control the conversation.

"A cottage is a dreary, cold place without heat. Have you ever been in one, my lord?" she asked quietly.

"Yes. I have been in cottages on occasion."

For a while she said nothing, and as they stared into the fire she reached up occasionally to wipe a tear from her face with a slender finger.

Jonathan sat by the girl and couldn't take his eyes from her. He studied her whole appearance—the thick raven curls, the sapphire eyes moist with tears, arched brows, the beautiful mold of her face and body.

For the first time in his life he felt a despondent gloom seep into the inner fibers of his heart and soul. This girl before him stood for value that he had seen in no one before. Her very life radiated something indescribable, something beyond his understanding, and he was caught in it, somehow. He loved this elusive nymph with a love unknown to him before in his loose, vague ramblings. But she was beyond his grasp as long as William's claim to her remained. One hope, only, buoyed him up. That William would not return.

Chapter 5

Jonathan's concern for his mother was the main reason for postponing his migratory trip to London for one week longer. But Elizabeth was the other.

Elias Shaftsbury urged him to go as planned. "You can surely do no good here, my lord. It behooves us to be about the enclosing. Think of the wealth we are letting slip through our fingers. The London market is extending outstretched hands to us for food, and we have but to supply it. The open land can be cultivated this winter and lie as virgin soil for planting in a few months." Elias's eyes bulged and the vein on his forehead took on a bluish appearance.

"What about the villagers, Elias. They gather wood from the open land for fuel. What will they do if they no longer have access to the land?"

"Hire them to do the cultivating, my lord, and with the profits give them wages. Let them buy coal—or logs in Dumford. Don't concern yourself with the lot of them. They're not worth it. There are plenty of men willing to work if they won't. We've got several farm properties now.

All we need do is cancel leases if necessary. Then that land will also be part of the estate."

"Can we do it by agreement with the men?"

"Of course not. They're stubborn as mules, my lord. You'd get nowhere with reason. Be firm. Get the enclosure bill. You're the dominant landowner around here, so get all the legal backing you can. Proceed quickly, for we need those enclosures now, my lord." Elias put more than average emphasis on that last phrase as he leaned toward Lord Giltham.

"I'll get to London when I can. But I must see how my mother fares before I leave." Jonathan found Elias annoying, aggravating to the core. Why the devil were the enclosures so all-important anyway?

Jonathan walked to his chambers and fell across the bed. He couldn't decide whether it was more of a heartache to have Elizabeth with him wherever he went—or somewhere else. Her presence was a constant reminder of what he couldn't have, a rare jewel shining and tantalizing but not attainable. And yet, to have her gone would be unthinkable, for he would yearn for her presence—her soft voice, her face and eyes.

Lady Giltham continued to improve, and Jonathan began to hope that she could be moved to London, by boat, if nothing else. There she could be nearer Dr. Sloane and under continual supervision. It remained for the doctor to give his permission, and that would take place the following week when he returned to see her.

Jonathan called Elizabeth to him frequently and spent hours with her in the library, or in the drawing room. Often he supplied her with volumes so that she could read them and discuss them with him at a later hour. When he was with her, the time flew by, and she, on occasion, would smile and relax in his presence.

Elizabeth found that she looked forward to those hours

with Lord Giltham. She was not anxious to see him leave the Hall, for it would surely be a lonesome place without him. And she began to look forward to his summons.

One morning early Jonathan asked Elizabeth to walk with him in the park, so she placed her cloak about her shoulders and met him at the entrance to the side portico.

The October morning was still. The martins had left and in their place was a silent void, except for an occasional night call from the brown owl inhabiting his domain in the woods or the carrion crow in stubble fields.

"The doctor will tell us next week if mother can go to London by boat. You, of course, will accompany her."

"Yes, my lord," answered Elizabeth, for the thought pleased her somewhat, never having been beyond Linton.

"You've been on the water before?"

"No, I have not."

"It's a pleasant journey, much more so than by coach, I must say."

Elizabeth pulled her cloak more tightly about her shoulders for an occasional gust sent cold air about them.

"The gamekeeper tells me there is more poaching than usual."

"The villagers feel that since God put the animals here they should be shared—and not kept only for the rich to eat."

"But stealing!"

"Perhaps they feel it isn't that. It is more of an ancient right," she answered, keeping her eyes straight ahead as they strolled along.

"And you condone poaching?"

"I do not condone poaching," she said softly. "But if the villagers were permitted an occasional hare, they wouldn't be poaching. At present it becomes a challenge to outsmart the gamekeeper. Families are hungry, my lord. And their purses meager. Every morsel helps."

They walked on to the baulks, ridges of land between the cultivated fields, and here they stopped. Jonathan watched a man digging something from the ground. "What can that fellow be doing?"

"Pulling swedes, my lord."

"Swedes?"

"A large turnip."

"All of that ground is in turnips?"

"Yes. He'll use it for winter feed for his cow and pigs."

"And it sustains them?"

"Quite nicely. You could do the same with your cattle and not kill them off in November."

"How do you know all this?"

"My father has done it successfully for two years. In that way enclosure is not necessary. With four-crop rotation all of the land is in use continually, instead of leaving one third fallow each year."

"But can it be done successfully on a large farm such as mine?"

"Certainly."

"Elias says enclosure is the only answer."

"Elias is not a villager, my lord. There is much he doesn't understand. No one understands the land as fully as one who has always worked it."

Jonathan watched the girl closely, for she was as much a part of the earth of Giltham as any tree or shrub. She loved this land and her soul cried out to the villagers. Her fight for the wretches was as intense as Elias's was against them. Was there anything that she didn't understand? He hated to admit that he knew next to nothing about his land, but then she undoubtedly knew that already. And yet she was patient with him.

"If you will notice, my lord, he walks in a straight line among the turnips," she said softly.

"And why is that?"

"He has planted them in rows, instead of broadcasting the seed. In this way he can keep the weeds from choking out his crop. It is a matter of economy for the yield is much greater."

"It seems a great amount of effort."

"Yes, truly it is. But fresh milk all winter from a sleek and healthy cow is the reward."

Jonathan studied the man for some moments—watched him pull the turnips from the ground and place them in a cart. "How is it that you know so much about the man's farming?"

"He's my father." Elizabeth kept her eyes on the man. She yearned to rush to help him. The work was hard and she was no longer there. Were the few shillings she earned at the Hall a just recompense for leaving the land she loved? She felt the moist earth in her fingers even as she watched. Then she turned. "I'd best return to the house."

For some moments neither spoke but moved steadily along through the park. When Elizabeth turned, glanced up at a bird in an oak, and stumbled slightly, Jonathan quickly slipped a hand through her arm to steady her. Once she stood upright again, her eyes glanced momentarily at the young lord, and their eyes met—the blue of hers with the deep brown of his. They studied one another for a slight space of time, looking into each other's secret recesses. She, suspecting that he would kiss her, lowered her eyes quickly and whispered, "How clumsy of me, my lord. Sorry." And they commenced walking once more.

Jonathan did not relinquish the hold on her arm, and although she felt uneasy about his grasp on her, she said nothing. Still she kept her eyes determinedly straight ahead of her. She remembered the bold kiss in the shepherd's hut and shivered slightly.

But the look that Lord Giltham had given her had its effect. Although she didn't want to admit it, Elizabeth found the sensation pleasing—something she had not experienced before—completely different from William's gaze, which brought no feeling with it at all. Even the arm that slipped more firmly into hers at this moment was a morsel of forbidden pleasure. Deep within her body a sensation awakened that was new and spread as a fever throughout her entire frame. Although she knew she should pull away, something hindered her from doing so.

Jonathan's racing heart urged him to clasp her arm more tightly, but he would not risk the chance of having her run from him as she had at the hut. He must bide his time, and wait, yes, wait—for William. When he thought of his friend returning and claiming her for his own, he sickened and clung to her as if he never wanted to let her go. And this time she did not run.

The week was gone before either realized where or how it went, and the time for departure could be delayed no longer.

Jonathan's valet packed his boxes in preparation for the London journey. When all was in readiness, Lord Giltham spoke a few words of parting to Elias and went directly to his mother's chambers.

"I'm happy to see you sitting up today," he said, planting a kiss on her pale cheek. Then he sat on the edge of her bed and looked into her eyes. "Now if you are good and follow the doctor's orders, you will be well enough to travel by water shortly and join me in London."

Lady Giltham sighed. "I hope so, my dear boy, I truly do. The thought of being here all winter is repulsive to me beyond description."

"But you have a good nurse. Elizabeth is attentive and capable. She can read to you, play for you, discuss books. The time will pass well enough."

"Hmph. I want to be in London for the season. Dancing. Not here with a nursemaid."

"Perhaps you shall, yet. I am hoping for it."

Tears gathered in Lady Giltham's eyes and spilled over onto her face. "One's life is altered so in a few months' time. Who knows what the year may bring." She reached her arms about her son's neck and clung to him as if she wanted never to release him. Her daughter, Carolyn, was gone from her—happily married to Lord Richmond—and Jonathan was the only loved one close to her. They must build the estate to enhance both their positions. A wealthy widow was even more attractive to London society. "Get the enclosure bill through as soon as possible so the estate will be even larger."

Jonathan shook his head, tired of his mother's forcing this issue. He changed the subject, hoping to please her. "Carolyn will be here shortly to spend some time with you. She is returning from the continent next week."

"Yes, but I will still miss you." She leaned back to gaze at her handsome, fair-haired son. "You need a wife, Jonathan. Find one in London this winter. One from a good family."

Yes, he thought as he listened to her words, *one who can bring a large income into the estate is what you really want.* But he remained silent. "Let's just get you well. That's my first concern; the other can wait."

"But not too long."

Jonathan shrugged and rose. "We will be together soon—either here or in London."

"Good-bye, Jonathan. Take care of yourself."

Jonathan smiled and left the chambers.

Elizabeth was choosing a book from the library when he entered and pushed the heavy door closed behind him.

"I am leaving now, Elizabeth," he said. "But I hope to see you and mother in London shortly. If not, I promise to return in a month or so to see how you both fare without me." He allowed a slow smile to crease the lines of his face.

Elizabeth raised her eyes but not her face as she felt his

hands on her shoulders.

He whispered softly, "I will miss you. I can't tell you how much I've enjoyed the pleasant hours I've spent with you, Elizabeth."

He continued to look into her eyes, those beautiful blue eyes that shone so brilliantly beneath her black lashes. He was sure he detected a tear lodged there—a lonely crystal of liquid formed on his behalf. This look would have to sustain him in the weeks to come—serve as an incentive to better himself. He wanted desperately to fold his arms about her for the last time as a remembrance to cherish through those long dull hours listening to the debates and speeches in Parliament.

At last he lowered his face and planted a solitary kiss on her forehead. "Take care of mother, won't you? I can't leave her in better hands."

Elizabeth nodded slightly. "Good-bye," she whispered. She watched him turn, move toward the door, and pause for a moment before he departed for his coach.

For some minutes Elizabeth felt a choking in her throat. Even though she returned to perusing the bookshelves, it was some time before she could see clearly enough to select a volume that would interest her through the intermittent long afternoon and evening hours.

She refused to admit to herself that she was promised to one man when she cared for another. "Oh, God," she whispered in the silence of the room, "work it all out as you see fit."

The first frosts spread their silent lace during the night and covered copse and hedge alike, stinging the elms and willows, the ash and sycamore.

Lady Giltham called to Elizabeth just as the pale light of day covered the earth with a hazy gray film of gossamer. "What time is it, Elizabeth?"

"The clock struck eight a short time ago."

"Carolyn may arrive today so I must be ready. Bring me my toilet case."

Elizabeth put another log on the fire and moved Lady Giltham's chair closer to the hearth as the lady brushed her hair and pinned it in place.

"Let me know the moment she arrives. Alert the servants, do you understand?"

"Yes, my lady."

By three o'clock the coach arrived, was announced, and Lady Carolyn Richmond entered the front passage with a great flourish of silks and laces. She was followed by a maid, a nurse, and a small child who at the age of four was a miniature of her mother.

The servants clustered about, fawning and patting and clucking at the infant with such dainty phrases as, "dear wee lamb," "angel child," and the like while Elizabeth turned and walked briskly to Lady Giltham's chambers.

"Your daughter has arrived, my lady."

"Well, show her in, please. Hurry I tell you."

But before Elizabeth could move beyond the chamber door Lady Carolyn brushed past her with only a momentary curious stare. Her face was held high in the air with no audible sound whatever to acknowledge Elizabeth's presence.

Elizabeth returned to her room, but she left the passage door slightly ajar. As she sat with her mending Lady Carolyn pulled the door between their apartments closed with a bang.

"Carolyn, my dearest." Lady Giltham drew the young woman to her.

"I'm sorry for the delay but our ship was a day late in sailing, and my husband was due back in Parliament. Diana and I came on without him. What does the doctor say about your health?"

"I must remain in bed and get a minimum of exercise."

"And you won't go to London this winter?"

"By boat if Dr. Sloane permits it."

"Where did you find that new waiting maid I just passed?"

"Jonathan had her brought to me."

"Jonathan?" Carolyn raised her face higher, looking down at her mother's drawn face. "You watch that girl, for I've seen her kind before. She's too pretty to trust. She'll be after Jonathan—if she hasn't been already. I warn you mother. Take care."

Lady Giltham was stunned. "Indeed, you are mistaken. She is a mere servant."

"Just remember what I said."

"Fortunately he's in London," Lady Giltham whispered.

"Well, then, I have good news. My husband's cousin will be with us in London. A pretty little thing and the daughter of Lord Crannybrook. I'll have Jonathan married by spring, I give you my word. But when can you go to London, mama?"

"Dr. Sloane says I can go by boat whenever I care to as long as I don't overexert. But," she added, "Elizabeth must come with me."

Lady Carolyn scowled. "You'll regret that. She's sure to be a conniving little thing—all of them are."

Lady Giltham was quite sure her daughter was mistaken, but she would be alert to the matter nevertheless.

Chapter 6

At sundown the White Hart Inn took on fresh mirth and joviality as the men of Giltham gathered to rest their weary bodies from planting and quench their thirsts with the innkeeper's home-brewed ale. In these moments of relaxation they shared bits and gleanings of news in and about the countryside. Tonight was no different.

"Sure as my name's Samuel Digges," said the thatcher with an air of great knowledge and importance, "they's agettin' ready for somethin' big up at the Hall. It's like as not they'll be a hedgin' our holdings afore the year's out. They's done it o'er in Dumford and the poor villagers is a starvin' and sellin' out and goin' to the factories."

James Shaftsbury, Elias's brother, watched the gathering with a sombre, thoughtful eye. He was a man important and respected in the village and kept good order—firmly allowing no drunkenness and making a strict practice to never drink with the customers. It was his full determination to remain on good terms with everyone in the village.

He kept an alert eye, as well, on Robert, the small serving boy who sat on a low stool beneath the massive oak beam of the fireplace and kept a steady cranking at the turnspit. The boy was an orphan taken from the parish workhouse in Dumford so he could earn his keep and not be chargeable to the parish coffers.

The 10:00 P.M. stagecoach was due in at the yard in half an hour. As Shaftsbury moved to the fireplace to make certain the large sirloin of beef was done he saw the door swing open and two very genteel men entered the room. Without being told, the servants scurried to be of service, taking care of their bags, coach, and horses while the innkeeper personally attended to their needs.

"Gentlemen," he said bowing, "I am at your service."

"We'd like a private room for dining and a bed for the night."

"Yes, sir. Quick, Robert, brandy and hot water in the private room in back for the gentlemen." Shaftsbury bowed to the men again as they followed the small boy across the brick floor to the dark, low-ceiled back room.

In a few minutes James entered cautiously into the private room carrying generous portions of hot savory beef and pudding. The taller gentleman had removed his coat. The diamond pin on his cravat caught and reflected the glowing embers of the fire with a flaming brilliance that attracted James's eyes in short snatches. But he was careful not to show too much interest.

"Your bags are in your room, gentlemen. If you wish more drink, I've a stock of fine liquors." He nodded and left the men to their quiet conversation.

When, at last, the men asked to be shown to their chamber, Robert lit a candle, took some linens smelling of aromatic lavender, and marched ahead of the men to the rooms above. Then, ever so carefully, he removed their boots and cleaned them with the alacrity of one whose livelihood depended on the performance. The gentlemen were much amused at his antics and rewarded him generously with more than ample tips.

The innkeeper waited impatiently for the boy to return below. When he showed his small frame descending the staircase, James set a bottle wrapped in cloth on the table, motioned for the child to sit, and proceeded to cut a generous slice of beef. Robert knew what was coming. He was filled with dread but he dearst not refuse.

"Take this to my brother as you have before, Robert. Gorse can go with you. Remember now, go quietly."

The boy shook his head, and when he put the last bit of meat into his mouth, motioned for the big dog to follow. James put an apple tart in his small hand and handed the bottle, with care, into his other. "If you drop it, I'll send you back with another," the innkeeper warned severely.

With pounding heart and eyes round as a doe's, the boy clung to the big dog and moved forward a few steps; then he stopped and turned to look into James's eyes. "The ghosts, sir, are they not out on moonless nights?"

"Of course not. There aren't such things as ghosts. I told you that. Now be off with you and no more of this nonsense."

Robert went off into the night as bidden but was totally unconvinced.

The road to Giltham Hall was one mile long but, at night, it seemed twice as long and would have seemed more lengthy still without the lights burning faintly in some of the cottages along the way, which appeared as pleasant friends, telling Robert not to fear.

When he finally arrived at the Hall, Robert took a small pebble out of his pocket and carefully threw it against the pane of Elias Shaftsbury's window. Then he waited.

In a moment the steward's face was peering out at him. Shaftsbury motioned that he would be at the door as soon as possible. A little while later, when the rear door opened slightly, Robert slipped the present in through the opening.

"If you say a word to anyone about this, you'll go back to the workhouse, Robert," Mr. Shaftsbury whispered. "Remember that."

"Yes, sir, I won't say a word."

As swiftly as he came, Robert disappeared into the night with his big companion.

Elias stood motionless as stone for a few moments until he was sure that no one had seen him come into the passage; then, as cautiously as he came he moved stealthily back down the passage and slipped unnoticed into his chamber. He stood by the door momentarily to listen for any sound that might lend itself to suspicion.

But there was none. All was silence. He clasped the bottle to him and carried it to the candlelight to remove the cloth and search the surface. At the bottom were the marks, 8 2 Lon C.

Elias smiled, and he placed the bottle behind the low stool before he blew out his candle. With a flourish of his hand, he replaced his nightcap on his head and climbed into bed.

When the following morning dawned the innkeeper rose, bathed his face with cold water from the pitcher and basin on his table, and pulled on cold heavy boots. For a moment he stopped by the guests' door to listen for stirrings. Then he descended cautiously to the large room below.

Through the bay window the first rays of morning sun were relentlessly prodding the thickness of the fog to make their way into the bleak interior. Quickly the innkeeper hurried out through the back entrance and into the stable yard.

The outside air was chill and damp and laden with thick swirling fog, which in moments engulfed him completely.

Two servants were moving mutely about the courtyard in preparation for the guests' departure at the hour of eight. James Shaftsbury nodded and disappeared within the stable. Then one by one, the servants followed the signal.

In quiet whispers James said, "Saddle my horse and let it be known that I had business in Crumpeton. Be extremely civil to our two guests."

"Yes, indeed, sir. We can be very civil to two fine gents as they is, sir." And the men proceeded to prepare the innkeeper's steed.

James mounted and the animal's hooves clattered slowly across the cobblestones, past the huge elm whose majestic foliage swept the yard with purple morning shadows. A glance backward told him that all was quiet in and about his inn. He was well pleased.

For about a mile James rode steadily along, watching the fog beginning to lift by varying degrees above the roadside grasses and foliage hanging heavy with liquid. Beyond the turn in the post road, he veered sharply to the left and followed a ragged, overgrown roadway until it shifted and angled between huge oaks and groves of beech.

From this point the innkeeper pressed his steed forward at a faster gallop. Beams of sunlight burst through the fog to light up patches of deep ragged grasses and presently the unkempt woodland gave way to thick meadows and a gently rising hillock. Beyond loomed a dismal gray structure—lichen covered and crumbling. A vestige of roadway led faintly to what was formerly a grand entrance to the now-vacant mansion, Shaftsbury Hall.

The innkeeper dismounted and whistled softly. From the south side of the house a low whistle answered in return. James led his steed to the entrance and tethered him alongside a sleek black horse that had arrived there before him.

"You're right on time. How did you manage it?"

"I told them I was riding the farmland to check on the

sheep and hogs."

"I'm at Crumpeton." Both James Shaftsbury and his brother Elias burst out laughing—smug and secure that their clever maneuvers had so easily and surely deceived the fools about them.

They walked together through a heavy oak door into what was formerly the kitchen of the old estate and pulled out from behind the decaying fireplace two cloaks of black wool and two pairs of dirty old boots. Each set about dressing himself in the strange outfits, adding, lastly, gray woolen caps to the tops of their heads.

"Are the guns keeping well. Show any sign of rust?"

"None in the least, but I might consider putting them in the chamber at the Hall," said Elias.

He reached inside a mouldy chest and pulled out a heavy darkened wrapping. The men unwound the canvass layers and studied the contents.

"They seem in good condition to me, but I think you are right, Elias. They should be in a warmer place from now on." James tried the flintlock of the pistol, examined the bore, and searched for signs of rust. When he was completely satisfied that all was working as it should, he laid the firearm across his horse's neck.

"We had best be on our way. My men will see that the chaise doesn't leave ahead of time."

"I hope they're to be trusted."

"They know if they give us any trouble they will go straight back to the workhouse as fast as I can sign the paper."

"And that boy?" asked Elias as they moved along the patches of ragged woodland toward the turnpike.

"You needn't have the least fear. He knows he'd get no beef or tips at the workhouse." James laughed softly. "You know, Elias, I am beyond reproach and a respected man in the village. No one would suspect me."

The horses started through the matted growth that masqueraded the roadway.

Elias smiled. "It will be better if we start putting the next money in another London bank. It's not good to make our accounts large."

"We will soon have enough for a herd of sheep. They always did best on this land."

"Yes, they did very well, indeed," Elias answered. "I can't leave Giltham Hall any too soon. I despise working for other men as a servant."

Before the brothers reached the post road, they urged the horses through an old, abandoned apple orchard. The hazy rays of sun shone on the gnarled branches, which lay bare and void of leaves. At a spot where the trees terminated on a rise of ground, the men dismounted, unrolled bundles, and threw them carefully over their horses' backs as a covering. Then they fastened them securely underneath the animals' bellies.

Elias applied a large patch of powder on his horse's forehead and drew his mask over his face as James was busy giving his steed similar changes of disguise.

They grew tense. Each man pulled his horse nearer to the road and put his gun on the horse's neck. From their vantage point they could see a distance up the post road and easily distinguish the vehicle when it came, for the fog was lifting more rapidly now.

They waited about ten minutes. Then they heard it: the first sounds of horses' hoofs pummeling the roadway beyond. Soon the rumble coming toward them from the direction of the inn became increasingly louder.

When the coach approached and thundered past and around the bend of the road, Elias led out in strong pursuit. In seconds he drew alongside the horses, aimed his pistol high, and shouted for the driver to halt or be shot. James drew up beside the chaise and pointed his weapon directly at the passengers. The men within the coach had been taken by such extreme surprise that they failed to reach for the pistols that lay on the seats beside them.

Gradually the team of horses came to a halt.

"We want your money and valuables. If you reach for your guns we'll fire so throw them on the road."

Slowly the driver raised his weapon and threw it onto a clump of grass while those in the coach did likewise.

"You in the coach. Get out."

The two gentlemen were very much alarmed at the suddenness of the assault and moved awkwardly to oblige. With their hands in the air, they seemed uncertain as to which way to turn.

"Put down your money and jewelry. Be quick about it." The men obediently threw down what they had, but the taller one hesitated to remove his diamond pin.

"Your pin, throw it down," demanded James in a manner that caused the taller of the two men to acquiesce.

When the brothers were satisfied that the travelers were thoroughly parted from their wealth, Elias motioned for the passengers to reenter the coach. "Move on," he shouted to the driver.

The chaise lurched ahead with great haste and was soon out of sight while Elias and James snatched up the money and jewels and hastened to disappear into the apple orchard with their prey.

As soon as the brothers were safely hidden they tore off the masks and counted their gain. Two hundred pounds. But the prize that crowned James's delight was the diamond pin—glimmering in the sunlight, catching the rays with intense brilliance. A gem unexcelled.

"I saw it on him last night when he entered my inn," said James. "You should have seen the way it caught the glow from the fire."

Elias shoved their newly acquired gain into a small bag

and both men removed the disguises, wrapping them in the horse coverings and hiding the pistols underneath.

From where they mounted, James and Elias remained silent until they reached the dark secluded covering of the ruins of Shaftsbury Hall. Then they howled with unchecked laughter at the success of their adventure.

Chapter 7

It was a bitter winter with the gray weepy skies hanging heavy and low, dropping flurries of snow, which were caught in the wild winds and whipped against barren black branches. In the ridges of the fields the partridge and carrion crow searched the stubble for bits of grain and an occasional small pebble.

Elizabeth kept the fire burning in her mistress's hearth in an attempt to dispel the pall of gloom that hung about the Hall. Lady Giltham's strength had failed to return, and she had not been able to bring herself to make the cold trip by boat to London, for she felt a continual chilling in her bones.

The woman sighed. "Jonathan should be coming in three days, shouldn't he?"

"Yes, my lady."

And he would come. Just as he had done every month since he had departed in mid-October. Lady Giltham lived for those visits from her son. The universe orbited around those few days that he spent with her, sitting beside her, talking to her, telling her the latest London gossip, and bringing the latest books. Yes, it was all she lived for.

The church vicar had called daily to cheer her and relate further spine-tingling tales of the latest bold adventures of the highwaymen. He had related these, of course, to warn her to keep doors bolted. But finally she had absolutely forbidden him to bother her, as she called it.

"He's such a miserable bore, either frightening or just plain dull. Tell him I'll call him when I want him," she had said.

Again Lady Giltham sighed. "The parties and balls are at their height now. Everyone always invited us in times past." The woman turned her face to the far wall and closed her eyes while the tears seeped out, swelled, and trickled down the side of her face. The bitterness of it all stung as gall. *I'm too young for this,* she thought with rancor.

Then Lady Giltham turned her head back to the hearth and studied the girl sitting there with her head bent over some mending. *Can it be that she is the conniving little thing that Carolyn claims? If that is so, she hides it well.*

True to his word Lord Giltham arrived home in three days by boat to avoid the rampant robberies—stiff from cold and happy for the warmth of a blazing hearth.

"You saw Carolyn and visited with her?"

"Yes, mother."

Lady Giltham was anxious to learn about the meeting with the young Lady Crannybrook so she began to pry. "Did Carolyn have guests?"

"Yes, but then Carolyn usually does. I wonder at her ability to endure them all."

"Who were they?"

"An uncle of Peter Richmond's as I recall. And another family."

"Who was the uncle?"

"Crannybrook," Jonathan answered dutifully.

"Does he have a family?"

"A daughter."

"Pretty?"

"I guess." He shrugged slightly. "But tell me. How are you feeling?"

Lady Giltham realized that she'd get no more information from her son. The meeting of the young lady was apparently not the instant love affair that Carolyn had anticipated. The woman breathed deeply. She couldn't be there to encourage her son, much less choose a suitable wife from the eligible young ladies this season. So she changed the subject.

"What about the enclosure bill?"

"That sort of thing takes time. You must be patient. There is much talk about the war with the colonies and the rise in costs that are resulting. Nasty thing, this war." Jonathan glanced into the fire and wondered about William. He slumped slightly. At this moment his only desire was to see Elizabeth, to listen to her soft voice, and watch her hair shine in the candlelight. He remembered the vow he had made to keep her from his mind. It had been useless. He kept rushing home to be with her, in spite of the realization that he should do otherwise.

As soon as his mother dozed he went to Elizabeth's door and knocked softly.

The girl looked forward to his visits more than she cared to admit, taking greater care than usual with her appearance when his visiting time drew near. Her heart beat a little faster when she heard the soft knock, and she tried not to move too quickly to admit her visitor.

When Jonathan saw Elizabeth, she looked as beautiful as ever in the firelight, proving once again that his thoughts of her had not gathered fantasy beyond truth and imagined greater beauty than was actually there.

"Elizabeth," he whispered, "I've missed you. Have you been well?"

"Yes, my lord."

"You are a little pale. I fear the hours as mother's nurse are too much for you. Let me hire someone to relieve you."

"No. Please. It's not necessary for I manage well."

"I will judge that for myself after I have examined your face more closely. Mother is not looking well, is she?"

"Not too well, my lord. But when spring comes and she can go out-of-doors, her spirits will rise, no doubt. She is weak."

Jonathan stared into the fire, and then turned to look at the girl near him.

"What about the enclosures, my lord." She refused to look his way but kept her eyes on the fire or on her hands.

"Well, I haven't done anything about it yet, I admit."

"But the notice on the church door."

"Um. That was Elias's idea, called it a 'courtesy,' as I recall."

Elizabeth said nothing but continued to stare into the fire. Courtesy was not one of Elias's traits. He had other reasons, she knew.

Jonathan sat upright and turned to face the girl before he spoke again. For some moments he studied her and wished he could claim her. "Have you heard from William?" he asked at last.

"I got a letter today, my lord."

"Is he well?"

"He claims to be. He's eating well and is impressed with the colonists' type of fighting. He doesn't say what that is exactly, other than it is copied from a method used by the Indians."

Jonathan should have been happy to hear that his friend was well but it only tended to depress him. *After all,* he thought, *he is there—and maybe for a long time—and I am here. I have Elizabeth to myself, and I mean to make the most of it.*

The wind howled mournfully outside and rattled the panes, and the drafts seeped into the room, frigid and unwelcome.

"Let me pull your chair closer to the fire as it seems to be getting colder," Jonathan offered.

Elizabeth rose and together they pushed the chairs nearer the blaze. But before Jonathan seated himself again he gave his chair a shove nearer the girl's.

"Tell me more about London," Elizabeth said softly.

"It's an exciting place, really, with so many people—rich and poor alike—all thrown together. People hurry here and there. The houses are row houses, mostly, with great chimneys that belch out smoke over the entire city. Carriages and foot travelers are everywhere, and hawkers call out for passersby to buy their wares."

"And you prefer London to the country?"

"Not necessarily, but it is a change."

"Have you ever seen a place called the Foundry?"

"No. What is it?"

"You have heard of Mr. Wesley, the preacher?"

"Yes."

"He uses it as a meeting house. Many come to hear him, I'm told."

"Yes, so I've heard." He reached over and gently touched the sleeve of her gown while he studied Elizabeth's face in the firelight. "Did you like the books I brought you the last time I came?"

"Yes, my lord. The writing is excellent and the plots hold interest. Your mother has enjoyed them immensely. They have been an excellent means for her to pass long hours."

"Elizabeth, won't you call me Jonathan?"

"I think it is best that I do not."

"But just when we are alone?"

"Forgive me, my lord, but I cannot do it."

Their eyes met for a fleeting moment; then she lowered hers quickly and stared into the fire once more.

"I've missed you, Elizabeth. I must admit it, right or wrong. I just wish that—" Here he said no more but allowed his hand to move downward and touch the fingers that lay cool and still on the arm of her chair.

The girl knew she must not permit the privilege, but the touch of his hand on hers was a pleasure that she enjoyed even though she attempted to pull away from him. He would have none of it and clung tighter still so that she leaned her head back and closed her eyes.

"I must admit to you, Elizabeth, that I do not look forward to William's return. At times, I almost wish he wouldn't." By now Jonathan turned and watched her closely for the reaction that the words would bring.

"Oh, my lord, you mustn't even think thoughts such as those. You can't mean them."

"I'm afraid I do."

At this Elizabeth rose and attempted to leave for she felt guilt at allowing such folly to continue. But he would not relinquish his hold on her and drew her to him instead, folding his arms about her and placing his face against her hair.

"You must know that I love you," he whispered. "You must."

The harder she struggled to free herself the more tightly he held onto her until she remained quiet. He felt her sobbing against his shoulder—quietly, softly, subdued. Until with a mighty effort, she freed herself and cried, "It cannot be. It cannot." She ran from the room and from the man she could never marry.

Chapter 8

The letter came in March on a day when the air was brisk and the smell of rain was everywhere, cooling and refreshing and blowing away the dreary dregs of winter. The sun struggled with the cumulus clouds, whispering past masses dark and threatening on one side and white and promising on the other. Every stalk longed to burst forth swollen shoots to bathe the countryside in delicate tints.

The thought of war on such a day seemed remote—an impossibility. Yet dying and killing were taking place at that very hour in a distant corner of the world known as the colonies.

William's letter forced this reality into Elizabeth's quiet existence. He lay wounded in North Carolina and was being sent back to England.

"I received a shell in my leg," he wrote, "and have been recuperating. But I will not be able to fight again, so it's time I return to you as I promised."

Elizabeth slowly folded the letter and placed it in her small case. How would she feel about seeing him again?

And how would Jonathan receive the news? As the wife of Jonathan's friend would she be able to be with Jonathan again without feeling pain?

Elizabeth knew that Jonathan had purposely delayed the enclosure bill to please her. But what would he do when she left Giltham? Would it no longer matter to him that the people were at the mercy of his whims for their very existence? She sighed. She must pray that it would not be so—even in spite of Elias.

The steward moved about the house and the fields with sullen anger. No one could please; no one could do his job right or quick enough. Elias was dubbed "The Tyrant" by everyone remotely connected with him.

The cottagers feared for their properties as never before, for Elias watched and waited—as hawks study their prey in readiness to swoop down and devour—for the remotest excuse to cancel their leases.

Elizabeth wondered where he spent his days, where he went when he sped away before daylight, and where he headed after dark. *He's a strange one,* she thought. *Surely he's up to no good.*

Not long after the April rains began, Jonathan sent word that he was returning to Giltham Hall for another visit. The months back in London had made him realize how much he needed Elizabeth. His whole existence had become centered around these brief visits home, as spokes from a hub. The pleasant liquid days of April lifted his spirits, buoyed them to new heights, for he determined to put William from his thoughts as if he did not exist at all.

The clouds parted as Jonathan and his valet approached the Hall, and for a while the sun burst through an inky patchwork of gray to shine on the fresh-bathed earth beneath. New green was everywhere and as Jonathan allowed his eyes to sweep the familiar landscape he saw her. She was following the carriage path onto the walkway that led through the park beyond.

Jonathan motioned his valet on and raced down the roadway to catch up with the girl. The gentle wind billowed her cloak as she walked. When he was within a few feet of her, he called out softly, "May I walk with you?"

Elizabeth slowed her step and closed her eyes for a moment before turning her face and looking into Jonathan's sparkling eyes. "My lord."

He stepped forward and placed his hands on her shoulders. Elizabeth looked down, but the man gently took her chin and raised her face upwards before she turned away.

"Elizabeth," he whispered, "I love you."

The wind blew pale waves of hair across his forehead, and he looked so very handsome. Still she shook her head firmly. "Don't, please, don't."

Again he seized her by the shoulders. "But if William doesn't return—"

"He is returning, my lord," she said.

Jonathan couldn't accept her statement as true.

"He's been wounded and will be returning to England as soon as he can," she explained.

Jonathan felt trapped by an iron vice from which he could never escape. *How am I to go on existing without her?* he wondered.

The pair moved on through the park without speaking. On either side the wind blew through sporadic patches of yellow primroses, and the daisies nodded their heads. Overhead the blue swallows flitted and darted in erratic flight and the nightingale sang its pleasant notes of spring love. But they neither saw nor heard any of it.

Again Jonathan ceased his walking and stood in Elizabeth's path, making it impossible for her to turn aside lest she step into sodden moss or rain-soaked weed. She stood as one deaf and mute to hear words that would be spoken for her ears alone.

"Elizabeth, I cannot, I will not accept losing you until I hear the marriage vows repeated by your own lips."

Elizabeth kept her face down, for the tears were welling and ready to release themselves. To speak would be folly. The lump in her throat was too great to allow the smallest of phrases to escape.

Jonathan pulled the girl to him and placed his arms about her. *This pleasure,* he thought, *may have to last me a lifetime.*

Elizabeth remained but a moment, before she pulled loose and ran toward the house without looking back.

After dinner Elias insisted that Jonathan meet with him in the library to discuss the finances of the estate.

"My lord, if you expect this estate to prosper you will have to push enclosures through fast. Your last gambling debt set the rent rolls back four months."

"Don't lecture," Jonathan cried angrily. "I'll do what I want. It's my money." He jumped up and began pacing the floor, walking back and forth to still his frustration.

"But it won't be for long at this rate. We bought the three largest farms out and that set us back. But if we manage well, my lord, we'll prosper beyond your wildest dreams."

Jonathan braced himself with outstretched arms against the hearth and looked down into the fire. *Everything is going wrong. I've no hope, no peace, nothing,* he thought. *If it was Handly who stood as my rival I'd not hesitate to grasp Elizabeth from his clutches. But, William. I cannot take from him the bride he has already claimed.*

"All right," he said at last, hitting the wall with his hand. "Go ahead and enclose the public lands. Start wherever you like." And he slammed the door on his way out of the library.

Jonathan couldn't face Elizabeth with his decision, so instead of calling her to him he went straight to his room and slumped in a chair by the fire. Two bottles of port were left on the table beside him, and he picked one up and drained its entire contents without even filling his glass. From his chair he took a hazy aim and smashed the bottle against the grate before he climbed into bed without bothering to undress.

Elizabeth read to her mistress until the lady's head nodded, and she stated the desire to be left alone to sleep for the night.

The hour was late but Elizabeth couldn't sleep. She hoped that Lord Giltham would call for her. Still she dreaded to meet with him again, for it was agony for them both each time they were together.

She undressed, brushed her hair, and sat gazing into the hearth. For a long time she considered the situation in which she found herself, the hopelessness of it all. *Oh, my Lord,* she cried, *I will abide by your will, whatever it might be. Take this situation and work it all out for I cannot. My eyes can't see beyond this moment and I am weary. So weary.*

By mid-morning the next day Jonathan and his valet had climbed into the boat that lay anchored at the river's edge and slid silently out into the current, leaving the Hall and the village behind. He slipped quietly away without bidding Elizabeth good-bye, for he could not bear the parting nor could he think about the pain of returning in June.

For hours Jonathan stared with unseeing eyes at the shoreline or another passing vessel, until he realized that they approached the city and maneuvered among countless blooms of white sails and masts from the tiny wherries to the barges. A jam of boats were departing or arriving from ports foreign and domestic, with holds packed with corn, tobacco, or degraded humanity headed for Australia. Jonathan longed for his own hearth as a dry haven.

The men moved the bags ashore and into a waiting carriage, pulling onto a street that looked more like a river than a roadway after its recent drenching and sparkled in the sudden appearance of the sunlight. Jonathan squinted in the brilliance.

The steady clomping of the horses' hooves lulled him into fresh pathos, for he knew that neither his hearth nor his club would offer solace beyond a few hours of warmth and diversion.

Jonathan undressed and ordered his bottles of port. He didn't stop drinking until his mind was numb.

From that time on Jonathan spent as much time as possible at his club. Days passed. Weeks drifted one into another. When Carolyn begged Jonathan's presence at her house, he went simply to escape the tedium of his life.

"Poor Jonathan," said his sister when she saw him, "you take mother's illness too hard. You must not brood so for your health's sake."

She watched him carefully as they ate dinner. By the time dessert was being served, she began to direct her remarks toward the subject that was uppermost in her mind.

"Young Aliza Crannybrook is a pretty little thing, don't you agree?"

"Yes, I will agree."

"And," Carolyn added softly, "she is taken by you, dear Jonathan. Besides, she is worth ten thousand a year, she tells me."

Jonathan looked into the fire but was unmoved.

"Oh, Jonathan, how can you be so passive about her. She is in love with you as sure as I tell it and is heartbroken that you hardly notice her at all!"

Again Carolyn waited for a response. "Promise me you will accompany her to the Chesterton's ball the end of May."

She kept urging him until he finally agreed to do it—to please her.

Jonathan tried in vain to show some interest during the

final sessions of Parliament. But as he sat in the richly paneled hall that last week and listened to Lord Chesterton's incessant droning, he could take no more. He slipped from the room and made his way to the street.

How far he walked—or where—he couldn't remember, for the area was unfamiliar. But when Jonathan leaned back against an old building for a moment he heard singing. Inside, a huge gathering was standing, harmonizing until the notes echoed from the ceiling. He'd heard nothing like it before. At first he moved on, but the singing drew him as a strong cord. He slipped inside to an old deal bench in the rear to listen.

As soon as the singing ceased a small man ascended to the rough pulpit. Jonathan rose to leave, but the words from the man's mouth held him back, for he spoke as a gentleman, yet in plain terms, of God's love and forgiveness. Nothing in his memory equaled the man's eloquence or facial expression as he spoke.

The days Jonathan had idled away in taverns and gambling houses, the money he'd lost and the selfish decisions he'd made flooded before him. This man's words spoke of something more than this: a life dedicated to serving God.

Such a simple, lofty ideal would have seemed ridiculous to Jonathan if it hadn't been for Elizabeth. Her quiet faith witnessed to the reality of this man's words.

The young lord was touched and would have stayed to hear more. But he glanced about him at the common gathering—the poor clothing and the gnarled hands—and the reality of where he was intruded upon his emotions. He slipped from the room quietly, realizing that he had visited the Foundry Elizabeth talked about and heard the preacher, John Wesley.

Jonathan kept walking until he found his club but he'd not forget the look on Wesley's face. He would never forget that, or the words he had spoken.

The late May evening was freshly bathed in a warm shower of drops, the air balmy and sweet-scented with pansies and sweet williams and roses. Jonathan got out of his coach and was escorted into the main passage to wait for Miss Aliza Crannybrook to descend from above. He paced the floor for a moment. When he turned, she placed her dainty foot on the top step and descended the stairway with her powdered hair piled high. Her white silk gown fitted low over her shoulders and billowed from her waist to the floor.

"Dear Jonathan," she cooed when she curtsied and stood next to him, lifting her big brown eyes to his face.

"Aliza," said Lord Giltham, lifting her hand to his lips. It was a limp thing of white flesh, scented and jeweled and extending from a plump arm that pulled back coquettishly.

Jonathan took her hand and led her to the waiting carriage.

Lord and Lady Chesterton received the guests as they were announced—he with his stiff unbending reserve and she with a slight smile that added a touch of melancholy to her otherwise sad, doelike eyes.

After the usual greetings had been exchanged, Lord Chesterton said, "Eleanor is leaving early to return to the country. I would like to ride home with you if you have room in your carriage."

"Of course, sir, I'd be honored," Jonathan replied.

"The affairs of state should be finished a day early. We can leave the morning of the thirtieth of May if that's agreeable."

"Certainly. The thirtieth it will be." Jonathan saw the line of guests behind them mounting so he and Aliza moved into the gathering.

Aliza was her tantalizing best in a crowd and approached everyone with her prize in tow. "You know Lord Giltham, of course?"

Jonathan breathed a sigh of relief when the music commenced and he was able to escape the close scrutinous looks the dowagers shot his way from behind glasses about the room.

When the partners dispersed and were handed refreshments, Carolyn came over to where Jonathan stood. "My dear brother, I must congratulate you on your excellent taste in partners for the ball. She dances like an elfin princess."

Jonathan smiled graciously. "Yes, so she does."

"Oh, Aunt Carolyn, you are so sweet," cooed Aliza. "If I am anything at all tonight, it is due to the handsome escort I am with, I assure you."

"Such a modest angel, she is, Jonathan."

Jonathan nodded a yes to his sister, but he thought to himself, *How lovely Elizabeth would look in a gown of silk. This evening can't end soon enough.* Still he forced himself to smile and attempt to enjoy himself for Aliza's sake.

When Handly approached him a couple of days later at the club and congratulated him on his wealthy catch, Jonathan was truly annoyed. *What's Aliza telling London now?* he wondered. *Certainly not the truth.*

Chapter 9

The rains continued during the last week of May, but days were growing brighter. The nightingale sang from the thorn hedge; the bees hummed their busy song and drank nectar from the hawthorn flower. From every corner sweet scents of blooms and sounds of bird calls blended to give rise to fainting spirits and fading hopes.

In the quiet of the night Elizabeth was uneasy. Perhaps it was a foreboding, but it hung over her and caused a restlessness. She rose to get a drink of water from her pitcher. None was there, so she made her way silently down the passage to the kitchen for water and was returning past the library when she stopped.

Why she should have noticed it at all was a thing of mystery. *I remember drawing the drapes myself after everyone retired,* she thought. *The one on the right would not draw properly, and it was a bother for some minutes. I'm sure I had closed it all the way, but now it's open.*

Elizabeth turned to move silently back to her chamber, but in doing so she saw a slight movement and a small light flicker and disappear. She froze to her spot against the wall and stared in stunned amazement as the movement of a man, sinister and black against the moonlight, reached a hand toward the drapes and closed them.

Suddenly everything was dark as a vault. Her eyes became sightless once more, straining and aching against the blackness of the passage. She was numb with fear as a frozen thing unable to move—scared lest she should draw attention to the very spot on which she stood, glued, unmovable. Elizabeth's ears strained to hear any movement that would betray the intruder's whereabouts.

Soon she heard the slight muffled sound of hands moving with heightened sensitivity along the passage wall and a soft padded step that finally faded into deathly silence.

The passage clock boomed the quarter hour and shattered the intense tomblike stillness to shake her from her reverie. She uttered a startled cry. Gripped with a renewed fear of being found in the passage, she groped her way frantically back to her chamber and went directly to bed, shivering as she fell into a troubled sleep.

When the light of early morning broke through her windows, Elizabeth wondered if the events of the night had really taken place. A slight haggard look was all that remained of the past night. Elizabeth rose and dressed quickly; then she walked briskly down the passage to the kitchen for a cup of hot water. She stopped momentarily to peer questioningly into the dawn-bathed interior of the library.

A strange compulsion drew her into the room, but a careful, fleeting scrutiny satisfied her desire to detect a misplaced object or a telltale footprint. There was nothing. Each carefully placed vase, book, candlestick was as it should be.

"Good morning, Miss Bardwell," called a voice from the library entrance.

Elizabeth turned sharply. "Good morning, Mr. Shaftsbury." She folded her hands and glanced toward the bookshelves, aware that Elias's beady eyes were upon her.

"You are looking for something?"

"Yes. I want a book of poems for Lady Giltham." Elizabeth turned directly to the shelves and began looking for the book, hoping that she appeared calmer on the outside than she did inside.

For a fleeting instant the girl wondered if she should mention the strange incident of the night just past, but she thought better of it. Instead she reached for a book, and walked from the room. Elias followed and disappeared in the opposite direction down the passage.

Elizabeth wished desperately that the master would arrive soon. Something was amiss at Giltham Hall, even though she couldn't prove it.

But by nightfall there was still no sign or news of Jonathan, and she grew uneasy. Even Lady Giltham seemed restless. Elizabeth did what she could to make the woman comfortable before going to bed herself.

The moon was covered over by racing black clouds, and within two hours the wind howled and the rain beat hard against the window, shattering both the silence and Elizabeth's sleep. When Lady Giltham groaned slightly from the next room, Elizabeth rose from her bed and went to the woman's side, studying the lady's uneven breathing and allowing her mind to wander first to Lord Giltham and then to William.

When the woman's breathing returned to normal, Elizabeth returned to her chamber but she could not sleep. Again she wandered out into the passage. As she approached the library she thought she heard a faint sound—a groan—and her body tensed with curiosity.

Surely it must be the wind, she thought. But again she heard a faint groan. This time her steps inched toward the library door with extreme caution, for there was a dim light in a crack by the fireplace.

Elizabeth moved slowly into the intense blackness of the room. Her heart beat until she could feel the pounding of it in her mouth, and yet she felt compelled to move nearer, cautiously maneuvering about the spots where she recalled furniture. In spite of her precautions, she accidently stumbled over something on the floor and fell against the cherry desk, knocking a vase over.

She smothered a cry. Instantly the light went out in the crack, only to appear again, fully lit and shiny beneath the face of Elias. All the grotesque, hideous features of his face shown in that small beacon and he looked as a devil itself.

"So, you come spying on me, do you?" he snarled. His visage was frightening in the light, and he moved steadily toward Elizabeth who stared unmovable at the sinister figure approaching her.

"You want to see where I came from, do you, wench? Well, I'll show you," he said. "If I so desire I can leave you there, do you understand?"

Elizabeth nodded and felt her body on the verge of utter collapse. Elias held the candle so near her face that she felt the heat of it against her flesh, searing the skin. He grabbed her arm and shoved her toward the paneled wall.

Suddenly Elias pressed a spot on the wall and the whole panel moved. He pushed her into the narrow black cavern beyond.

When her eyes adjusted, she saw a blood-stained figure lying on a reed mat on the floor. The eyes opened and the ghostlike figure gasped, "Elizabeth."

She stared at the man, bent over him. "William! Is it really you? What has happened to you?"

"Grazed by a shell, that's all," said Elias. "But he needs care. Get some hot water from the kitchen.

"And if you breathe one word to anyone, I'll see that

your father has an unfortunate accident," he snarled. "Now get going quickly and bring a cloth."

"Don't leave, Elizabeth," the man called out pitifully in slurred weak tones.

"I'll be back, William, as soon as I get hot water. I promise." She glanced at the contemptible wretch holding the candle and headed for the kitchen. What Lady Giltham would do if she called and got no answer, Elizabeth couldn't guess, but she knew that William was wounded badly and needed help.

Her body was stiff with fear and rage at the audacity of the brute to threaten her father's life, but she must not take any chances that his words were merely shallow, empty threats.

If Jonathan would just return, I could go to him for help. But would he even believe me?

There was a red glow with a few hot embers in the kitchen grate, so it took little effort on her part to coax the ashes to flames with the help of wood chips and small logs. Elizabeth placed a little water in the kettle so that it would heat quickly. While the liquid began to bubble, she tried to reason out the strange event.

What had caused William's wound? Why didn't Elias just call for a surgeon and place the man in a bedroom?

Elizabeth got a clean cloth and a dish. After she poured the hot water into the vessel, she added more to the kettle so there would be a supply when she returned.

She lost no time in carrying the requested materials to the library where Elias ushered her roughly into the black passage once again. Elizabeth refused to look at the man but bent silently over William and began to bathe his wounds.

"Oh," groaned William, "the pain is beastly."

"This will help, and I'll be as gentle as I can," she whispered to him. While she bathed the ugly wound she studied his white face. *He's aged greatly,* she thought. *His eyes are sunk and his face is thin. His whole body is leaner than when I saw him last.* When he stared up into her face she could not help but think of Jonathan and compare the two. Even as she worked she felt a pang of regret that this was the man who would marry her.

William groaned again, "Don't leave me, Elizabeth. Stay with me."

"I'm here and I'll take care of you, I promise. But I'll have to go for more water. Just lie still. Can I get you a little food? Some tea?"

"Yes, tea, that would be good," he whispered.

Elizabeth rose and faced Elias. "You'd better check the mistress, for she'll wonder where I am if she calls."

"You check her, and I'll stand in the passage. But not one word to her, I warn you, wench."

The girl brushed past him in anger, too agitated to speak.

Lady Giltham breathed steadily, so Elizabeth hurried to the kitchen, wondering how she'd manage both William and the mistress until Jonathan returned. *And if Elias doesn't get a doctor for William, how can I get a message to his parents?*

Elizabeth cut a slice of meat and prepared a cup of tea, adding sugar to make it sweet; then she carried the food and hot liquid back to the library.

"Drink this, William," she whispered. The girl placed her hand carefully under his head and let the tea trickle down his throat. He revived somewhat and ate the meat bit by bit as she placed it in his mouth; then he lay back and let Elizabeth bathe his wound once more.

"Is the shell still in his arm?" she asked Elias.

"Of course not. Now don't ask questions, or it will go badly for you, understand?"

She bit her lip to control her anger and concentrated on washing the wound.

William was relaxing somewhat with her beside him, and

the food strengthened him so that his glazed eyes stared into her face. "It has been so long since I've seen you," he whispered. "I thought of you all the while I was away. I was on my way here to you when this rogue robbed—"

"Silence!" demanded Elias. "You'll say no more. Do you understand?"

William closed his eyes, refusing to acknowledge the man's presence.

"Don't try to talk now, William. Can I get you more tea—a bun, perhaps?"

"More tea, yes."

Elizabeth rose. "Can't we get him into one of the bedrooms? It's so miserably uncomfortable for him here."

"I'll take care of his bed. You just get that tea," Elias snarled.

Elizabeth glared at him. She could have reached up and raked her nails down his gaunt cheeks. But she held her peace for she must think of William and what she could do on his behalf. Now she knew Elias would never call a doctor, not as long as he was around and William could implicate him.

By five o'clock she grew weary. "Try to get some sleep now, William, and I'll rest, too. Then I'll be back to attend you in a while."

"Don't leave me," he begged.

"I'll lie down here in the library and I'll be near," she whispered. This seemed to satisfy the man so he closed his eyes. She walked wearily to the sofa and lay down. In seconds she dropped into a deep, exhausted sleep.

When early morning light came sifting through the window, Elias awakened Elizabeth and instructed her to keep the servants from the library. "I will tell the maids to clean on the second floor and remain out of sight."

Elias opened a small shaft to allow air into the tunnel and turned to Elizabeth. "I will get some breakfast and you return to Lady Giltham. But, I warn you, one word of this and both you and your father—as well as this soldier—will meet swift ends. With you out of the way, no one will know of the soldier, will they?" He put his beak of a nose near hers and squinted with a despicable look of revenge. "Do you understand?" he snarled through his clenched teeth.

"Yes," she answered coldly, "I understand."

Lady Giltham was calling for Elizabeth when she entered the room. "Where have you been?" she asked.

"I'm sorry, my lady, I did not intend to be gone so long."

Lady Giltham sighed angrily. "You're no more dependable than the rest."

The words cut Elizabeth to the quick for she strove to serve faithfully. But what could she say that would placate the lady. The harm was erasable and no true reason could be given.

"Help me sit up."

A fire burned brightly and Elizabeth breathed a sigh of relief that the woman didn't question her more intently about her absence. While she helped Lady Giltham with her dressing gown she tried to think of a way to get a message to William's parents. She truly feared for his life if he was left in that horrible hole many more days.

"You have something on your mind, young woman, what is it?" snapped the lady.

"I did not sleep well, that's all."

"Are you well?"

"Yes, my lady. I'm just tired." Elizabeth helped Lady Giltham pull her black gown over her head. The taffeta slipped easily over the lady's head, and as Elizabeth tied the ribbons in place she had a sudden idea.

"My lady, the hems of several gowns and the seams need stitching. Shall I take them to my mother to mend?"

"Are they that bad?"

"Yes, indeed."

Lady Giltham was not convinced. "We'll look them over before I give my consent."

Elizabeth swallowed and hoped she could get a few of the seams and hems undone while her mistress was resting.

When Lady Giltham was settled comfortably, Elizabeth slipped away to get breakfast for her mistress and then take some food to William.

The tunnel was closed when Elizabeth finally opened the library door and went in. She stared at the wall. There was no sign of life whatever.

Has something happened to William? she wondered.

She put the tray down and ran to the wall. *No one would believe my word against Elias's. They would say I was mad. Oh, God, let him be here!* Elizabeth rapped sharply on the wall and waited. She hammered again and listened, straining every vessel of her head so her ears were sensitive to the slightest vibrations from the inner compartment.

An ever so slight muffle of sound ensued, and the wall shifted gently—just enough for Elias's beak and beady eyes to detect whether the arrival of an intruder was fair or foul. When he saw Elizabeth, he adjusted the opening to allow her entrance. She picked up a cup of chocolate and toast from the tray and took it into William who lay still as death on his makeshift pad. He turned his head slightly in the candlelight and looked at her through glazed eyes.

"I brought you some breakfast," she whispered. "Come, eat, so you can keep up your strength."

While he ate she studied the wound and found it an ugly red—a vile, sore, festering thing that needed attention soon if he was to live. The young man looked imploringly into her eyes, and she smiled to keep his courage up. Then while he ate and she did not need to face Elias, she spoke, trying to keep her voice steady so she would not reveal her plans.

"My lady wants mending sent to the seamstress. Dare I

leave long enough to deliver the dresses?"

"No," was Elias's instant reply.

"Then how are they to get there?" she asked heatedly.

"Quiet, wench, I'm thinking." He moved toward the narrow, moldy stairway as if he could concentrate better there.

Soon he returned and stared at the girl's head as she bent over the soldier. "All right, the clothes can go, but I want to see them first, do you understand? I'll inspect them; then I'll send a footman to make delivery."

"I'll fetch them," she said without looking up to face Elias. It was all she could do to keep her hands steady as it was. "Can I get you something else, William?"

"No," he said weakly, holding onto her hand. "If you could stay with me, I'd—"

"I'll return in a short while. As soon as I can get away, I promise."

"Knock three times when you come back and make sure you're not followed," warned Elias.

Elizabeth rushed to the lady's room. "While you prepare your toilet, my lady, I will go through your dresses and look for those that need repairs."

The girl moved into the robing room and picked up scissors. She pulled the gowns from the wardrobe, and then very carefully slit and pulled threads on two gowns at the hems. Swiftly, she cut the material at the arm seam on the third.

For a moment she searched for some white muslin but found none, so she ran quietly to her room and brought back a thin petticoat from which she cut a narrow strip of the cloth. To avoid suspicion she called out to the lady, "I'm looking through your other gowns as well—as long as we are doing this job."

Elizabeth worked as fast as she was able, praying that all would go well. As her fingers flew she thought of William.

She had not looked forward to his return, not since Jonathan's declaration to her.

But there is nothing I can do, for Lady Giltham would never allow Jonathan to marry me. Nor would father be pleased, she reminded herself. *Jonathan doesn't even pretend to be a Christian.*

When she finished the last of her work, she piled the gowns together and whispered a silent prayer that the lady would consent to her sending them off immediately.

"Here, my lady, are the ones I found." She held each up to the woman for her scrutiny. Elizabeth's hands shook ever so slightly.

The woman studied the hems and seams for a time before she opened her mouth to speak at all. "I can't understand how all this could be," she whispered.

"Perhaps you caught them on your heel or a rough place in the floor."

"Take them—just take them—and get them back as soon as possible, for I need them." She leaned back on her chaise.

"Yes, my lady, I'll send them this morning." Elizabeth hurried into the next room with a lighter heart. *Thank you, Lord,* she breathed. *Now get them past Elias.*

Elizabeth hurried to the library with the three dresses over her arm. She carefully closed the door and knocked on the carved oak three times. Elias opened the wall a crack.

"While you look the dresses over I'll call a footman," she said, handing the dresses to him. "Lady Giltham wants them taken to the seamstress immediately."

"I'll call the footman," Elias snapped and he picked them up to examine by the window.

The day was overcast. No sun broke through the dense layer of cloud formation and mists to reveal any undue bulges in the material or facilitate inspection of minute flaws or details.

Finally Elias looked up. "Put the gowns on the table in the hallway while I go for the footman. Then go on back to the mistress."

"But I have directions. I usually take them, you know."

"All right, tell me."

"I'll write them down so neither of you will forget." Before he could object, she picked up the heavy garments and followed Elias. He opened the library door cautiously and peered about him before he gave her the signal to exit.

Elizabeth returned with a note and handed it to Elias. The footman waited silently while the steward studied the scrawled message to see if he could detect anything unusual about it. Then he handed it to the footman along with the gowns. "Take these to Mrs. Bardwell, the house across from the inn. Use the cart."

"Yes, sir."

Elizabeth turned and with a prayer of thanks on her lips walked back toward Lady Giltham.

The lady was staring at some zenith in space when her waiting maid walked into the room. "It's so gloomy and I'm depressed for the house is so dreary and stale. When will my son return to me?"

"Soon, my lady, I'm sure. Would you like to rest nearer the fire?"

"No, just let me be."

The great hall clock chimed the hour, and its music reverberated through the passage as a great ominous messenger. Elizabeth went about the room tidying everything in sight to relieve the tension building up within her. *Would her mother find the piece of material she had placed inside of one gown's hem? Oh, God,* Elizabeth breathed to herself, *work it out somehow.*

Chapter 10

The footman rapped on the door of the carpenter's cottage, handed the gowns along with the note to Mrs. Bardwell, nodded slightly, and left.

Martha Bardwell carried them to the settle and studied the piece of paper before she examined the dresses. *That's Elizabeth's writing, but done so poorly, as if scrawled in a great hurry.* She paused to look at the gown. *My stitches should not have come apart like that. The Lady must have caught her gown on something–a heel, perhaps—and Elizabeth says she wants them immediately.*

Apples were piled in a basket waiting to be washed and cooked before they became overripe. Martha debated which to do first. "Black is difficult to see at night so I'll do the gowns," she decided.

The sun shone warm and the air wafted mellow. Martha took her sewing into Matthew's workroom to sit near him, where the light poured in from the bay window bright and clear. "I got special work from the Hall and a note from Elizabeth. Her writing is not as good as it once was." She sighed as she loosed the remaining threads that held the hem in place.

"What does it matter?" said Matthew. "She seldom needs to write."

Martha didn't answer for she had her own thoughts on the matter. The hem was entirely loosed, and Martha pulled back the folded material to measure the one inch when she discovered a white inner band of cloth. The thin band had been inserted by someone, for she had not placed it there when she constructed the gown.

"How strange," she said half aloud. And then her eyes discovered some writing. She held the piece up and read. "Go to Chesterton Manor, Dumford. Tell Lord Chesterton his son is a prisoner of Elias Shaftsbury at Giltham Manor, and may be dying. Lord Chesterton should ask for me when he comes. *Hurry!* E.B."

"Oh, Matthew there's trouble at the Hall. That's why she sent these dresses in such a hurry."

Matthew put down his tools and moved over to his wife who reread the words again for him, very slowly and deliberately.

"Do you think Elizabeth is in danger, Matthew?" she asked when she had finished.

"I don't know, but she wouldn't send that message if it wasn't urgent." The two pictured the sharp evil features of Elias and tried to fathom an answer to this strange turn of circumstances.

"I'll get the horse." Matthew paused a moment and added, "Put some apples in the baskets and I'll carry them with me, just in case anyone questions the purpose of my journey."

Quickly Matthew headed for the small barn to the rear of the cottage. Martha followed shortly with the baskets, and Matthew tied them in place over the horse's sides.

The carpenter ambled his horse along, taking no chances

in case Elias was watching from the Hall. But when he was out of sight he urged the beast at a good pace, following the turnpike road into Dumford.

It was a market day with many about, so Matthew went to a stall to inquire the direction to Chesterton Manor.

"Follow the road beyond Dumford toward London. It's the great house on the right—about two miles—with iron gates and tall pillars at the entrance."

Matthew nodded and headed his animal toward that direction. The air, when not warmed by the sun's rays, blew cool against his face. But he was unaware of the elements.

His eyes studied the scene ahead for the first glimpse of the gates or the house, restraining himself from urging the horse at a pace beyond its endurance. Then around the bend in the road he saw them: pillars and the gate, just as the man had said. They were set in from the road a short distance. Matthew turned his horse to the right and drew up to the small office window.

"Who approaches?"

"I'm Matthew Bardwell, sir. I've an urgent message for Lord Chesterton."

"He's not here."

"Then I must see his lady. It's an emergency."

"Wot kind of emergency?"

"Lord Chesterton's son is ill at Giltham Hall."

"He's in America fightin'."

"Not now. He's at Giltham Hall."

Matthew had such a straightforward look about him that the gatekeeper called a small boy to direct the rider toward the house.

The lad ran as the wind and approached the rear entrance where he knocked for admittance.

A footman opened the door and peered out. "Wot d' ye want?"

"A man, sir, to see her ladyship."

The footman eyed the rider for a moment, studying his poor clothing as Matthew dismounted and hitched the horse to a post.

"I've an urgent message for Lord or Lady Chesterton. It's about their son William," Matthew explained, looking directly into the footman's eyes.

The footman hesitated for he wasn't entirely convinced, but he motioned the man in and led him down the passage to a small room. Here he spoke softly to someone for a few moments, and then he returned with the butler.

"You say you have an urgent message for Lady Chesterton. On what business?" asked the butler.

"Her son William is at Giltham Hall and ill."

"But he is not in this country."

"He is, sir, and at Giltham Hall. Please, it is urgent."

"I'll take word to Lady Chesterton. Wait here, please, and be seated."

Matthew nodded and watched the butler disappear down the passage while the footman sat in a convenient spot where he could keep a watchful eye on the visitor.

Matthew leaned forward with his arms resting on his knees. All this seemed so unreal to him. He didn't wonder that he was being questioned by the men at Chesterton Manor.

Soon Matthew heard light steps and a swishing of taffeta approach. He rose to meet Lady Chesterton.

"You claim you have a message for my husband and me?"

Matthew looked into the large troubled eyes of a woman in her forties. She was small and pretty with dark hair falling in curls about her shoulders. There was something hauntingly familiar about the woman.

"My lady, I have an urgent message for your husband concerning your son William."

Lady Chesterton studied the carpenter's earnest face; then she motioned him into the room where the two men sat near the fire. "Sit down, please."

"My daughter, Elizabeth, is the waiting maid of Lady Giltham at Giltham Hall."

At the name of Elizabeth, the lady drew in her breath slightly, for she had heard her son speak of the girl.

"My wife is the lady's seamstress, and this morning Elizabeth sent this message to my wife in the hem of a garment." Here Matthew pulled the thin strip of cloth from his pocket and laid it out on the lady's lap for her to read.

For a few moments she studied and restudied the message. "But how can it be?" she asked. "We have not had word that William was even in England."

"I know nothing except what the message says."

"Why didn't Lady Giltham write the note? Surely she would know he is there."

"I can't answer that for I don't know. But I do know this. Elizabeth would not write this if it wasn't urgent. She is dependable."

Lady Chesterton rose and paced nervously between the fireplace and the window. Both her servants stared after her and studied Matthew carefully.

"You are a servant at the Hall?"

"No, madam. I am the carpenter in the village."

"And would Elias do this sort of thing?"

"If Elizabeth says so, he would. She has never been given to falsehood."

The lady sighed and continued to pace. "Leave the cloth with me. I will send a servant to search for my husband, for he is not due home until tomorrow. We will come as soon as we can. If William really is ill—"

Then she stopped and looked at the men. "Joseph, get a horse and ride the turnpike toward London to search for Lord Chesterton. He will be in the Giltham carriage. When you find him, tell him to hurry home. It is urgent."

Her great eyes were filled with anxiety and fear for her

son. She moved to the window and stared out over the fields in the direction of Giltham.

The air turned cold by afternoon and blew fresh and chilling from the north, bending smoke ribbons into twisted wisps that trailed into nothingness and disappeared. Jonathan studied the fields and meadows and occasionally the slumping form of Lord Chesterton whose nodding gray head bounced against his cravat and turned first one way and then the other as the carriage bumped along the turnpike road.

He thought about his wasted, senseless life—the girls who gave up their virtue too easily, the money he lost at the tables—and loathed himself. Next to Elizabeth it was all a sham. His life was worth nothing without her. She was steadfast; her faith strong. Oh, if he could possess a faith that held firm when all else was crumbling.

While Jonathan thus mused he heard a commotion outside the carriage, and the horses drew to a standstill. He grabbed the pistol beside him and held it in his lap; then he pulled as close to the window as he dared and stared out beyond the coach.

Lord Chesterton raised his head. "Oh, we must be home already."

"Hush," Jonathan whispered. "We are stopping, but I can't tell what the devil it's about. Keep calm and get your pistol ready in case it's highwaymen."

A rider approached the carriage and called out. "Is Lord Chesterton inside? I've a message from her ladyship."

At this Lord Chesterton leaned against the carriage window and stared out at Joseph. "Eh? A message. Whatever about?"

The servant jumped from his horse and poked his head inside. "Her ladyship said to hurry home as fast as ye can. It's about Master William."

"He's hurt? Speak up, man, speak up!"

"Ye'd best let her ladyship explain, sir. He's at Giltham Manor and a prisoner."

"What do you mean, prisoner?" snapped Lord Chesterton. "What kind of nonsense is that?"

"Just hurry, my lord, and she'll explain." Joseph galloped off, leaving the stunned pair inside staring at one another in absolute unbelief.

"Can you make any sense out of what he said, Giltham?"

"None whatever," answered Jonathan. "The man's got something twisted. We'll know what in about another forty minutes."

But the coach seemed to move at an unusually slow pace. The wind and ruts all were base impediments to speed, holding up the flight. Those forty minutes seemed longer than the whole day combined. It was unbearable. Agonizing.

The wind increased with the darkening clouds, and rain began to pelt the carriage and fill the ruts with cold liquid that smattered the wheel with muddy foam. Trees bent before the onslaught. The men strained to catch the first glimpses of Chesterton gates. When the carriage finally moved through the ironwork and approached the front entrance, Lady Chesterton threw open the door to meet them.

"Now what the devil is all this nonsense about," Lord Chesterton asked. The water stood in a sheen on their coats while they loosed the buttons and stared into the lady's large frightened eyes.

"It's no nonsense, Alexander, come and I'll show you how real it is." The lady ran to the servants' hall with the startled men close on her heels.

From a drawer Lady Eleanor produced the thin strip of white cloth and laid it on the table for her husband and Jonathan to study.

"Who gave you this, Lady Chesterton?"

"The carpenter, a Mr. Bardwell, came this afternoon—"

"Matthew Bardwell—from Giltham?"

"Yes. That's who it was."

"Can you trust this fellow, Jonathan?" Lord Chesterton asked quickly.

"Absolutely, finest man in Giltham," whispered Jonathan. "But Elias. What's gotten into him? It's all so incredible."

"What about Elizabeth? Is she reliable?"

"Certainly. She wouldn't send this if it wasn't dire emergency. She may be in danger as well." Jonathan moved impatiently. "Let's take the horses, and get to Giltham as quickly as we can."

"What about a servant for added protection? Highwaymen, you know."

"Yes, take Joseph and the pistols."

"But I must go, too," cried Lady Eleanor.

"No, my lady, it will be necessary to use caution. We will have to ride in quietly at sundown." Jonathan headed for the passage and his coat. "We'll make plans as we ride. Hurry, sir."

"But can I follow in the coach, Alexander? If William's dying—"

"Get the surgeon and come in the morning if you like," Lord Chesterton replied. "Now, come, Jonathan. Let's go."

Lord Chesterton sent a footman for three fresh horses and the men galloped off toward Giltham.

Chapter 11

The rain had dwindled to a mist and ceased entirely as the borders of Dumford disappeared behind them. Ahead lay the turnpike road to the north. Already the afternoon was slipping away, and the men were eager to reach Giltham before dark.

"I'll ride into the carriage house alone, and you come a little later in case Elias is watching. There is a cover of woods to the north," Jonathan told Lord Chesterton. "If anyone asks why we don't have the carriage, say it had a broken axle."

As dusk approached Jonathan drew his two companions to a halt behind a stand of oaks and elms on the far borders of Giltham Parish.

"I'm going to ride on ahead. James Shaftsbury's inn is on the turnpike road, so continue on until you come to the first road beyond the inn, and then turn left. It will bring you in near the stables behind the house. Wait at the stables. I'll send a servant for you when it's safe to approach the house. But use caution, I warn you."

The men nodded and watched Jonathan ride off on the main road toward the Inn.

The young lord passed Matthew's shop and walked the horse at a leisurely gait to cause no undue alarm. He left the horse at the stables before walking to the servants' entrance. Then he paused. He considered his plan carefully and opened the door.

At first the servants didn't see him enter the kitchen, for they didn't expect to see him there at all, much less appearing at dark without a servant to welcome him or give him aid.

"My lord," cried the flustered cook when she saw him standing at the door. As she curtsied the heads of the others turned his way, and each gave a shocked gasp at being so suddenly intruded upon.

Jonathan ignored their dumfounded stares and walked over to the cook.

"May I see you outside a moment, please?" He motioned toward the open door.

The bewildered cook followed her master while the servants stared in absolute silence. "Nancy," she called over her shoulder, "watch that meat so it doesn't burn."

"Yes,'m," the girl answered, but she didn't take her eyes from the departing cook.

Jonathan pushed the door closed. "Is everything all right at the house?"

"All right, sir?" she asked. Her face displayed an incredible bewilderment. "Of course, my lord. Why wouldn't it be?"

"Is Elizabeth all right? Have you noticed anything unusual in her actions?"

"No," she said. Then she hastened to add, "Well, maybe a little."

"A little?"

"Well, sir, now that I think about it, she has been in

the kitchen at night which is unusual."

"Doing what?"

"She's been makin' fires and boilin' water, and she's lookin' tired and actin' a little on edge. But then with my lady and all—"

"And Elias?"

"Elias? Why to tell the truth I've not seen him for a few days. He has his meals sent to his room."

"I want you to listen very carefully and do exactly as I say."

"Yes, m' lord."

"Go in and tell the footman to find Elizabeth. Act as if you're very angry about something. When she gets here, tell her that you want to have something settled, and bring her out here to me. If Elias accompanies her, don't let him follow. Just get her out here to me. And act *angry*. Let everyone think you are going to scold her proper—alone. Do you understand?"

"Yes, sir."

"All right, go!" He motioned her impatiently away.

Jonathan closed the door except for a small crack and watched Matilda Henneson storm into the kitchen as a disgruntled rooster. "Martin! Go get that Miss Bardwell and be quick about it. I've got a thing or two to settle with that girl. Now be quick, do you hear?"

"Yes, Mrs. Henneson," he answered, hurrying out of the kitchen.

The minutes seemed as days until Martin returned with the girl.

As soon as Elizabeth appeared in the kitchen door, Matilda began her tirade. "So, you show your face, do you. Well, let me tell you a thing or two. We'll not have this out before the servants, no indeed. You just come with me beyond this door." Mrs. Henneson shoved the stunned girl through the doorway and closed it behind her.

Elizabeth stood and stared at the cook without a word, waiting for whatever outbursts were forthcoming, when Jonathan approached.

"Wait here until we return, Matilda."

When Elizabeth saw the master, she gave a cry of relief and rushed to him. He grasped her hand and led her to a nearby cover of shrub before she burst into tears and was pulled to his breast.

"Oh, I am so glad to have you here. I was afraid you'd not get my message."

"It's all right, Elizabeth," he said, holding her tightly to still her quivering body. "Lord Chesterton and a servant are waiting at the stables. Now tell me what Elias is up to." He felt her body tense against him.

Elizabeth pulled away and spoke. "Elias has William in a secret passage in the library. He's got a bad wound and needs a surgeon desperately. But Elias threatens me with my life and my father's if I tell. Oh, it's been horrible. Be cautious, my lord, for he'll kill William if you go near."

"What do you suggest, then?" he whispered.

"I'll go in to take William his supper. If you hide in the library, you can take Elias by surprise when he opens the wall. Soon it will be dark enough to get into the library unnoticed. But take care. He is a desperate man."

"Did Elias see you come out here?"

"I don't know. He may have followed me."

"Then you'd best go back. We'll get into the library somehow and we'll have pistols. Oh, Elizabeth, I've missed you," he said softly.

"And I you, but—" She bit her lip and turned suddenly, returning to where the cook waited by the door.

Jonathan followed. "All right, Matilda, continue your scolding—and make it convincing."

The woman threw open the door and shoved Elizabeth inside. "And, young lady, don't you forget what I said."

Elizabeth wiped the tears from her eyes and saw the passage door close slightly. Elias had indeed seen the leaving and entering, she was sure. But had he heard her exit through the outside door? There was no time to wonder. She must return to Lady Giltham at once.

When she left the kitchen, Elias grabbed her arm. "What was that all about?"

Elizabeth tried to pull away, but he twisted it even harder until she burst out, "Oh, I broke a cup. Stupid thing to get so upset about." Elizabeth was glad it was getting dark in the passage so he couldn't see her face as she talked.

"Get supper for you and Lady Giltham and a little for the soldier but beware, I warn you."

"Yes."

"By the time Giltham gets back tomorrow I'll be well away. So don't foil my chances tonight. I'll murder, I will," he hissed.

Elizabeth went to prepare the mistress for her supper; then she walked to the kitchen and put Lady Giltham's food on a tray. As she turned to go back through the dark passage, Jonathan called softly to her from behind the kitchen door. "Elizabeth."

"Yes, my lord."

He placed a warm hand on her arm and whispered, "We'll follow. Is Elias in the library now?"

"I cannot say, but I will go into the library to see. Keep out of sight and I will signal to you."

"We'll follow and go behind the draperies in the passage to wait." Jonathan squeezed her arm slightly and let his hand fall to his side while he nodded to the two men beside him.

Elizabeth moved down the passage and opened the door enough to study the room carefully before she signaled an entrance to the men. They slipped past her silently, and she pulled the door closed before proceeding toward the mistress's chamber with her supper.

Elias was carrying a box of some sort down the hall toward the side entrance, and Elizabeth drew in her breath at the man's form disappearing through the doorway and into the night. *He can't leave William in that hole,* she thought. *Where is he going? Is he sneaking away?* She would have run after him but Lady Giltham called.

"What are you waiting for, Elizabeth. Bring my supper at once before it is stone cold."

"Yes, my lady."

"You are acting so strangely. What are you about?"

"I thought I saw something, that's all."

"You have a vivid imagination. I'll be so happy to have my son home tomorrow." She sighed.

"Yes, I'm sure you will, my lady." Elizabeth tried to keep her trembling hands calm and her voice steady.

As soon as she could she excused herself and made her way back down the darkened passage to the kitchen. Quickly she picked up a tray.

"Aren't you going to eat with us, Elizabeth? We've a place set."

"No," she tried to control her voice. "I'll eat with the mistress."

"Hmph. This is wot happens to girls of low birth who are put in places of their betters."

"Oh, hush." Elizabeth tried to get the tea and food from the bowls to the dishes without betraying her extreme anxiety. As quickly as she could, she left the kitchen, trying to smile at the servants as she passed the table.

Oh, God, steady me, she prayed as she walked the length of the passage to the library. By the time she knocked on the library door and Elias opened it, she felt unnaturally calm. A sense of peace still surrounded her as she stood quietly watching Elias light a candle and shove the door closed behind them.

In the light Elizabeth searched the room for a sign of the men. There was none. She studied Elias proceeding before her. He was dressed for traveling in a suit of black wool, and held a candle while he opened the wall and peered inside.

"Now feed him and be quick about it."

Elizabeth placed the tray on the library table. "I'll give him the tea while it's hot, if you'll bring his food in a moment," she answered as she walked into the dismal passage.

Elias set the candle on the floor beside the boy and walked out to get the tray.

In an instant a slight commotion was heard and the master shouted, "Don't move, Elias."

Elias Shaftsbury stared at the three men who pointed guns at him, and ran into the passage. But Jonathan fired before Elias could get all the way down the moldy stairway that led to the outer exit. His body hit the floor hard, but no one moved to inspect his injuries.

"William!" cried Lord Chesterton when he saw his son lying on the floor.

"Is that you, father?" The words came from white lips that were barely able to form audible words.

"By heaven," Lord Chesterton cried in a hoarse whisper. "What has the madman done to you?"

Elizabeth sat in a crumpled heap beside William and watched as the men moved the boy from the damp passage onto the sofa in the library.

"Send for a surgeon, Giltham, as fast as you can!" Lord Chesterton shouted. Jonathan moved back to Elizabeth and helped her to her feet before he ran down the passage toward the kitchen.

Elizabeth studied the crumpled form of Elias, still inside the passage. Even in unconsciousness he made her shudder, for she expected him to rise up and snarl at her at any moment. His dark suit was absorbing the sticky blood that seeped in a nonstop flow from his back. Elizabeth ran from the room for more cloths.

In the kitchen Jonathan was giving final instructions to the servants. Each was put to a task of boiling water, making tea, or procuring cloths while one of them raced out into the night for the surgeon. The footman Norman was instructed to help Elizabeth in the library.

When Elizabeth returned with her basin, she saw Lady Giltham coming down the passage, calling angrily for her.

"Where are you keeping yourself? You know I can't be left alone. What are all the candles doing in the passage? Where's Elias?"

"Come into the library, my lady." Elizabeth took her arm and directed the lady into the library. At the sight of Lord Chesterton and William on the sofa, she gaped in bewilderment. "What is going on here?"

"Your son will explain when he comes back."

"He's here at the house?"

"Yes, my lady. Now if you'll be seated, I must attend to William—and Elias." She told the footman to try to stop the flow of blood from Elias's wound; then she set the basin on the floor and hurried for blankets while Jonathan brought in more candles.

"Jonathan! Will someone tell me what has happened here?" Lady Giltham cried.

"I haven't time now but I promise you there will be a full explanation shortly."

As soon as Elizabeth returned with blankets, the men removed the soldier's uniform; then Elizabeth applied cloths to William's face.

"Elizabeth, don't leave me. It's cold."

"I'm here, William, and so is your father." She continued to bathe his face and speak softly.

William continued to whisper until he fell into unconsciousness.

"How long has he been here like this?" Lord Chesterton asked in anguish.

"At least two days, sir." Elizabeth rose and brought the candle closer to the sofa where the young man lay pale as death itself. "I'll go for more water. The excitement has been too much for him."

Lady Giltham moved nearer and demanded to know why Elias was wounded, but before anyone could answer, one of the maids accompanied the doctor into the library.

"The surgeon is here," Lord Giltham announced.

"But how did you—?" Lord Chesterton was too stunned to speak so Jonathan finished the sentence for him—"get here so fast? Your wife sent him, sir. It's a good thing she did."

Everyone moved back so the surgeon could have room to examine William. He pulled back the cloth and found the ugly, gaping wound.

"Get boiling water, fast, and get a copper pot scrubbed and boiled."

"I'll see to it," said Lord Giltham.

Elizabeth knelt on the floor of the passage by Elias and helped the footman sponge the wound until she heard a faint groan from Elias's lips. Her pulse quickened at the revival of the man—a stirring of consciousness that brought back the memory of threats and scathing insults. But she remained until the surgeon and Jonathan came to inspect his condition.

Lord Giltham helped them get Elias to a bed in a small dressing room adjoining the bedroom they had moved William to, so the surgeon could care for both of them.

"Bring a fresh basin and cloths and put the water kettle on the bedroom hearth for easy fetching," the surgeon ordered. When this was accomplished, he added, "Let the footman remain with the man in the other room, but the rest of you leave until I call for you." He took a small vial from a bag, hesitated until the door closed completely, and then walked toward the fireplace to relieve the young man's pain and treat the wound as best he could.

Chapter 12

"What can the surgeon be doing for so long a time?" Lord Chesterton asked after a couple of hours had passed. Everyone except Lady Giltham was waiting in the library for word from the doctor.

"Come, sir, he has two patients to care for. It is bound to take time," said Lord Giltham.

After another half hour had slowly ebbed away, the footman came into the library with the message that Elizabeth and the copper kettle were wanted quickly. Jonathan helped the girl to her feet, and they and Lord Chesterton made their way to the second story once more.

"How is William?" Lord Chesterton demanded the instant they saw the surgeon.

"I won't know until morning, for infection has set in. Both of the men are in critical condition." Then turning to the girl, he said, "William's shoulder will have to soak until the infection drains. We will take turns at watching both patients and adding hot water to the kettle. Bring blankets to rest the young man's neck against the rim."

"Yes, sir." Elizabeth obeyed his orders, moving trancelike for numbness had pervaded her entire body and rendered her senseless to those about her.

The surgeon, with the help of Jonathan and Norman, the footman, arranged William in the awkward but desired position and instructed her to keep the water warm at all times to avoid chills.

"I will rest for an hour; then call me if I don't return to relieve you," the surgeon said as he turned to leave.

Lord Chesterton followed the surgeon from the room, still quizzing him about William's condition.

"Norman can continue to care for Elias. I'll stay with you to help," Jonathan said as he arranged two more chairs near the tub.

"But your mother, my lord—"

"I already asked Nancy to care for her needs," Jonathan replied.

"Would you ask one of the servants to notify my parents that everything's all right? They must be worried."

Jonathan agreed to send someone early the next morning.

William remained ashen, more dead than alive, and lay as an inanimate thing. *He cannot possibly feel the love for Elizabeth that I do,* Jonathan thought as he watched the still form. *Though I have to admit he's a better man than I am. Oh, God, I yearn to remedy that, if I could somehow.* He closed his eyes and rubbed his forehead in frustration.

The girl felt the water in the kettle and leaned back. "Your stay in London was pleasant, sir?"

"Disgusting would be a better term, I'm afraid. I haven't your ability to make myself either useful or sensible."

The master's statement reached the heart of the weary girl and dispelled exhaustion as a healing balm. The veil that had stood in the way of her talking about her faith had been pulled away by his words. She was now free to speak as she had desired for many months.

"But you can change your ways, my lord."

"That's simple for you to say, for you are good by nature."

"No, sir, I am not—nor is anyone."

"All right then, how?" he sighed. "If you knew my life, you'd not say that."

"Knowing your life wouldn't make any difference. All of us are unworthy at times. But God gave his Son as a way of escape. If we believe that Jesus is our Savior and truly repent, he will forgive us. It is that simple."

"I wish I could believe it."

"Take my word for it. He forgave me as a child, and forgave many others who asked him. It's the only way to peace of soul."

"Oh, Elizabeth, I wish I could—" He stopped abruptly.

"Ask, my lord, it's that close."

Jonathan studied her—the way she moved, the way her tired eyes sparkled with a brilliance when she talked of this forgiveness. *Why,* he asked himself, *must I love her? I want her so badly.* Then he chided himself for such a thought. He watched her care for the soldier and a jealousy crept over him, a deep cutting, sickening pain.

Elizabeth seated herself beside him again. As they sat in silence her head nodded with weariness and her eyes grew weighty.

"Come," he whispered. "Lie down on the chaise and sleep."

"No, I cannot," she said. But the urge was too great. Sleep overcame her as if accompanied by a great dose of laudanum. She permitted the master to arrange a pillow for her before she sank on the cushions and slept a deep sleep of complete exhaustion.

For two hours Jonathan grudgingly cared for the soldier and thought about Elizabeth's words. It seemed too simple, this prayer of forgiveness. And yet, he remembered a time in his childhood when he had seen John Wesley. Even when men pelted him with obscenities and rotten food, Wesley had seemed calm and at peace. His face had had that same look only a few weeks ago when Jonathan had heard him preach at the Foundry.

Is there truly hope for me? Jonathan wondered.

Soon the surgeon came in to study his patient and relieve those on duty. Jonathan left and went to his bed to sleep.

The next morning Lady Chesterton arrived at Giltham Hall and went directly to her son's room. Her husband was there, caring for his stepson.

"William, oh, William!" she sobbed as she entered the bed chamber. "What has happened to you?" She gazed down into the pale face of the son she'd not seen for months.

"He's much improved," Lord Chesterton said. "The surgeon was able to bandage the wound early this morning, the infection is drained, and he has taken food."

"Will he be all right?" The lady's eyes were large and frightened.

"The surgeon believes so. Now, come and be seated," he said. "Let me order you something to eat."

"Just tea. Please tell me what this is all about."

Lord Chesterton sent Norman to the kitchen. Then he turned to his wife.

"William told me this morning that two masked men robbed the carriage he was riding in toward Giltham. He struggled with the one. When he pulled the bandit's disguise off, he discovered it was Elias. The other man shot him, and he fell unconscious. When he awoke, he was in a secret chamber in Giltham Hall."

"Where is Elias now? Is he under guard?" Lady Chesterton wondered.

"Yes, he's in the adjoining room."

The lady gasped. "In there? So close to William?"

"He's not likely to move for he's wounded and seems to be getting worse rather than better. The surgeon says he's not fighting to live."

During the long hours of that day, Lady Chesterton left her son's side only to take some air and exercise her weary limbs on the causeway. She permitted no one near William except the surgeon or her husband and demanded that Norman be ever on guard at the door that separated the evil Elias from her son.

But the lady had little to fear from Elias. The discovery of his thievery had destroyed all his hopes of regaining his past wealth and position. He lingered until shortly past midnight the next night; then he drew his final breath. His body was removed to his own chamber to await burial.

When Jonathan rode to the inn to find James Shaftsbury, he was informed that the innkeeper was away and would not be returning. Nor did his servants know where he went. So Elias was buried with no family whatever in attendance and few to mourn his parting.

The sheriff from Dumford asked a couple questions about Elias's injury. Then he added hastily, "All involved in this man's death are cleared of any ill doing whatever. Elias Shaftsbury has received his proper punishment. Better than most highwaymen, in fact—dying in bed rather than dangling from a tree."

Before he left, the sheriff assured them, "We will do all we can to find his brother. However, I am afraid he has left England. I have heard that he withdrew sums of money and jewels from banks in the area and fled to France."

Even though Jonathan knew Elias Shaftsbury would have been hanged eventually, he abhorred the fact that he had fired the shot that led to the man's death.

In the passing days Elizabeth stayed out of sight of the

Chestertons and allowed them the full pleasure of their son's company. She felt no rejoicing in leaving Giltham Hall as William's chosen, and yet it must be. Her silence was assent.

Jonathan appeared often when she walked down the passages or went for a stroll in the air.

"Must you go, Elizabeth," he asked one day. He paused and studied the girl beside him as they walked along the carriage path toward the stables. "I need you here with me. You make up what I lack in judgment."

"But it cannot be, my lord. I am penniless and Lady Giltham would not approve. No," she said firmly, "it cannot be."

"None of these things matter to me."

"Please, sir," she said. Her voice was shaking and she felt the sobs rise in her throat. "God will work out his will somehow."

They moved beyond the stables, behind hedges and away from prying eyes, and the master reached over and touched her arm. He studied her face. "Elizabeth, tell me you do not love me, and I will not press further."

Elizabeth shook her head but would not look at him. "Don't ask me to answer, sir." She buried her face in her hands and shook with muffled sobs.

"Oh, my dearest—" He pulled her to him, and she remained a moment before she pulled away.

"I must return to the house, sir."

She turned and hurried back toward the house.

Jonathan watched her flee and felt a pain of despair. In his defeat he leaned against an elm for support, closed his eyes, and cried to God to forgive him for his rotten, worthless life.

Fill this void with hope and a higher nature, he pleaded. In the flood of yearning, he suddenly felt a warmth, a penetration of peace, almost a soft word spoken from beyond.

When he opened his eyes, it was as if he saw for the first time the world in all its beauty. For some time he wandered and thought and looked.

When Lord Giltham arrived at the Hall some time later, he saw the Chesterton carriage creaking around the arc of the carriage path toward the village. Who the passengers were, he could not ascertain. The distance between them was too great.

In an instant he was entering the front passage and encountered the footman with a box in tow.

"What is going on?" Jonathan asked anxiously.

"The servant and William are preparing for departure, my lord."

"He is able to travel?"

"Not entirely, but Master William is insistent and the surgeon would permit it only under his care." The servant placed the container by the front entrance and turned to face his master. "Lord and Lady Chesterton departed already. They waited for a while to state their gratitude, but when you didn't return they departed."

"Yes, I saw the carriage leave."

"Lady Giltham has been asking to speak with you, my lord. We've been searching for you about the grounds."

Jonathan nodded and walked toward his mother's apartment.

The lady was lying on her chaise and watching for him when he entered the room. "I can't believe what is happening!"

"Happening?"

"William is taking Elizabeth with him. He begged so—said he couldn't recover entirely without her help and he owed his life to her." She paused and stared into space. "Can it be that he intends more than he admits?"

"Would you approve of it, mother?"

"A marriage?" She studied her son for a moment before

she answered. "Well, it is highly improper, certainly."

"Does it matter if he loves her?"

"Love, hmph! What does a child of twenty know of love?"

"As much as one at thirty."

A knock at the door drew both Jonathan and his mother from their conversation.

"Come in."

Elizabeth appeared in traveling dress and cloak. She had never looked more beautiful than now with the sunlight from the window bathing her black hair with golden beams.

"My lady, I am ready to depart for a while. I am sorry to be going for I don't like leaving you like this. Nancy will help you while I'm gone." Her eyes rested for a moment on the master. "My lord," she said, "good-bye." She curtsied, turned quickly, and fled down the passage.

"Excuse me, mother. I may be needed to help transport William."

The surgeon directed the making of a carrying bed for William and arranged the blankets in the carriage to suit his fastidious requirements for travel. Then he directed the servants as they placed the young man in the carriage.

Jonathan desired a moment alone with Elizabeth, an instant to tell her that he had found peace, but too many others surrounded them.

When all was in readiness, Elizabeth glanced at Lord Giltham for a moment. Their eyes beheld each other in silence before she was helped into the waiting conveyance and the door closed between them.

Lord Giltham watched the carriage travel the turn of the carriage path and disappear beyond the Hall. He listened to the parting wheels as long as he could, and then turned and disappeared inside the Hall.

Chapter 13

As the carriage headed toward the turnpike Elizabeth turned to the surgeon. "May I stop for a moment at my parents' cottage, sir? It is on the main road through the village—across from the inn where the turnpike joins."

"Yes, we can stop for a moment, but no longer."

She nodded and settled back, watching the familiar fields pass before her.

It was not long until the surgeon saw the inn come into view, he called to his groom to stop. Quickly he helped the girl from the coach and into the cottage.

"Mother?"

For a moment only the ticking of the long clock was audible to Elizabeth's ears. Then she heard the scraping of a chair and her mother's voice called, "Elizabeth? Is it really you? Oh, my child what an ordeal you must have been through!" She threw her arms about her daughter.

"I am well, but I must see you and father before I go. Is he in the workroom?"

"Yes, come."

Matthew was putting the stains on a chair when his wife and daughter entered.

"Oh, father," she cried. "I had to see you before I left."

"Left?"

"Yes. William has asked me to go with him to help nurse him back to complete health—and stay there for a while." She studied the stunned expressions on her parents' faces once the full impact of her words settled into their understanding. "I shall return, but I don't know when."

"He is a good man, a Christian?"

"I spoke to him about it, father."

"It is not right. It must not be, child," said Matthew. "Be not unequally yoked is God's admonition."

Elizabeth's eyes filled with tears. "Trust me, father. I will not forget. Now I must hurry. The carriage is waiting, and I promised to stay but a moment." She turned from their sober faces and walked through the sitting room toward the front door.

"Elizabeth, wait. I have something I must give you." Martha Bardwell turned and walked to the fireplace, removed a loose brick, and pulled out a small linen-wrapped parcel.

"What is it, mother?"

"A jewel on a ribbon. It was on your leg when your father found you. It is costly. Do not lose it and wear it when there is occasion."

Elizabeth looked at the small linen parcel and then at her mother.

"I knew there would be a right time to give the diamond to you, and it is now. Wear it for it is yours," her mother said softly.

Elizabeth tucked the jewel in her bag, kissed her parents good-bye, and then turned abruptly and departed. She waved as long as the pair was in view.

Then she settled back against the seat to ponder the

strange situation in which she found herself. *How could such a jewel have been around my leg when I was a poor orphan of no consequence?* she wondered.

When Elizabeth found William staring at her, she blushed crimson and lowered her eyes.

"You will like the house my father has given me on the estate, Elizabeth. It's not large but it has good design and proportions. I've admired it since I was a small boy, because it is surrounded by great trees and shrubs and is at the far edge of the park."

"It sounds lovely, William."

"The lease for it will end in two weeks. Father told me yesterday. We can move in as soon as it is cleaned, say in four weeks."

The remainder of the journey William talked of the house they'd share and of tales of his boyhood on the estate.

When the carriage neared Chesterton Manor, Elizabeth interrupted William to express something that had been at the back of her mind since they left Giltham Hall. "Please allow me to wait in a small room until called for. As a servant, I cannot go in to them without their requesting it. And promise me that you will explain fully the circumstances of my leaving Lady Giltham."

"Very well, but you'll not wait long."

The surgeon went ahead to prepare the room for William's occupancy, but the servants waited at the door for Master William. When he came into view, they greeted him royally. Each curtsied or bowed and was truly happy to see the boy who had left over a year ago and returned a soldier of the war. After he was helped from sight, each resumed his duties with a buzz of excitement.

When Lord and Lady Chesterton finally gathered beside William's bedside, he immediately told them about Elizabeth.

"You brought her here, William?" his mother asked.

"She is Lady Giltham's maid?"

"Yes."

"But, why, William? I am capable of—"

"I love her. I told father about it when we were still at Giltham Hall."

Lady Chesterton was stunned. "A maid, William. You are in love with a servant?"

"She doesn't look like a servant to me, my dear," Lord Chesterton admitted. "Nor does she act like one. On the contrary she is a bright young woman, and she did save William's life you know."

"Yes. But marriage—"

"Please, mother, send for her and treat her as one of us."

"Very well." She left the room to make the request of a servant.

Elizabeth and the footman arrived at the door. "Miss Bardwell, my lady."

The girl stood in the doorway until Lord Chesterton raised his hand and motioned her into the room. "Come in," he said. "My dear, this is Miss Elizabeth Bardwell."

"My lady," said the young woman, and she curtsied. But she remained standing before them all until the lady gave her consent for her to do otherwise.

"How long have you been at Giltham Hall?" Lady Chesterton inquired.

"For nearly a year, my lady."

William studied the two women as they conversed and was somehow struck with the similarity, although he was sure his mother would deny it vehemently. *But,* he thought, *she will learn to love Elizabeth after a day or so.*

On the second day the surgeon came to rebandage his patient. Elizabeth and the Chestertons watched as the doctor dressed the wound.

"Well, my man, you heal nicely and if—I say IF, mind you—you take care, you may walk about for a while. You may even take supper with your family tonight."

"That's good news, doctor, the best yet," William replied joyfully as the doctor prepared to leave.

Once the doctor and his parents were gone, William grinned at the girl who would soon be his bride. "Did you hear! I can get up and walk around."

"For a while—if you are careful," she added quickly.

"Dress for supper, will you? Dress in your prettiest gown, and I shall accompany you in myself. You will have to get used to that you know."

Elizabeth nodded. Perhaps, in time, she would get used to it, as he said.

Before supper Elizabeth slipped out of the room to prepare for the evening. She bathed and chose her gown—a pale blue. Elizabeth took much time in arranging her thick raven hair, for the sapphire of her gown heightened the blue of her eyes. Tonight was William's special treat, and she'd not appeared at the Chesterton's table before. She wanted to look her best.

Carefully she studied the results of her toilette in a full-length mirror. But something was needed. A brooch, perhaps—a scarf or a touch of lace. The jewel, of course. Her fingers searched her bag and felt the small diamond wrapped in its layers of linen. She held it to the candlelight to study once again. Set in a gold filigree, the jewel hung from a velvet ribbon. It moved in her hand and the lights reflected a myriad of dancing beams.

"It's too rich for a servant girl," she said to herself. Again she studied her image in the mirror. *But there is something wanting in my appearance. I will wear it.* She placed the jewel about her neck and glanced approvingly at the result as the clock chimed nine.

Then she moved out into the passage. William stood at the bottom of the great stairway watching for her. As she approached, his eyes radiated his love for her. "You are beautiful beyond words. And the jewel. Where did you get it?"

But before she could answer, Lord and Lady Chesterton descended the stairway and stood before them.

"You are ready and waiting, I see," said Lord Chesterton. "Come."

Elizabeth turned toward the man and his wife. As she came face to face with them Lady Chesterton gasped and clung to her husband for support.

"What is it, my dear?"

The lady was ashen. She stood absolutely immovable—a dumb statue void of life itself.

"Eleanor!" Lord Chesterton cried again and again. He could neither move her to a seat nor bring her from her state of shock.

"Mother," begged William, "what is it?"

Lady Chesterton took a deep breath and released her husband's arm. She stared at Elizabeth and whispered in a voice barely audible to the ear, "Where did you get that jewel?"

"The jewel, my lady?" asked Elizabeth in surprise. "It was found wrapped about my leg when I was discovered by Matthew Bardwell as an abandoned infant," she whispered.

"Abandoned infant?" the lady whispered, refusing to be seated.

"Yes, my lady. My father discovered me in Lord Giltham's carriage when he went into Linton to get a chest to restore. No one claimed me, so the carpenter and his wife raised me as their own child."

"I cannot believe it!" cried Lady Chesterton over and over, weeping hysterically.

By now Lord Chesterton used great force to get his wife to a sofa where she continued to weep uncontrollably.

"Oh, my lord, I should never have worn the jewel. Forgive me. I shall remove it immediately."

"No," said the lady. "Stay where you are, for I must speak with you." Then she turned to her husband and William. "Please go into the dining room and commence supper without us."

"But, my dear, we can wait."

Lady Chesterton shook her head impatiently. "Please. Please do as I ask."

"Very well. If you insist."

Both Lord Chesterton and William stared in bewilderment but did as she bade them.

When the woman regained a reasonable amount of composure, she hung her head and whispered. "Elizabeth, you are absolutely certain about the jewel being on your leg when you were . . . abandoned? There is no way it could have come to your parents by other means?"

"No, my lady. My mother placed it in a linen wrapping and kept it hidden in a secret place all these years. When she learned that I was leaving to come here, she gave it to me."

Lady Chesterton looked up into the face of the pretty girl standing before her. "Tell me. Do you possess a marking on your body, a birthmark?"

"Yes, my lady. I have a small red mark on the right leg above the knee—toward the back."

For some moments the woman studied Elizabeth's face: the blue eyes, the smooth skin, the raven hair. Yes, the raven hair, especially. She trembled uncontrollably and rose to her feet. "You," she whispered touching the girl's hair, "are my daughter."

Elizabeth stared as one dumb. For minutes the room was without sound as the two women took hold of what that meant to each of them.

"Now if you will, please call the men back, for I must tell them, too."

Elizabeth moved toward the dining room, entered, and

stood before the men, silent as stone for a moment.

"What is it, Elizabeth?" cried William.

"Lady Chesterton wishes to speak to you both."

The men rose in unison and followed the girl to where Lady Chesterton sat on the sofa. Her face was wet with tears and she played nervously with her rings.

Lord Chesterton sat down beside her and placed a reassuring hand on her shoulder. "What is it, my dear?"

"This will be a shock to you both, but it must be said in your hearing." She drew a deep breath, her voice shaking and her lips parting. "Elizabeth is my daughter." She raised her head slowly to look at the girl, then at William, and then at her husband beside her.

The men gasped and stared in stunned silence.

When William overcame his numbed senses, he cried out, "What are you saying? It cannot be. She is to be my wife!"

"But it is the truth, William," she said. Then turning to her husband she looked into his ashen face and whispered, "I'm sorry, my dear, but I had a daughter before I married you. Yes, all these years I have lived with the guilt and the pain of not knowing what happened to her. I was told there had been a tragic accident. Her nurse fell into a rushing stream while holding her, and no trace was found of the baby."

Lady Chesterton allowed the tears to flow freely down her face. "Many nights I woke and imagined I was drowning just as I thought my daughter had."

She rose and touched Elizabeth's hair as she spoke. "I wanted to keep you, but it was not proper, my mother said. She forced me to give you to a nurse far enough away so that I would not see you. But before you were taken from me," the lady whispered hoarsely, "I placed the jewel—this jewel—on a velvet ribbon about your leg."

Lord Chesterton strode from his wife and the room, his

hands behind his back and his head bent.

William stared at his mother and refused to accept her words.

"I'm sorry, my son," she whispered. "But you have a sister, not a wife."

William bit his lip to stifle the bitter disappointment that blurred his vision. "Is there no possibility that you may be mistaken?"

"None whatever."

William walked from the passage back to his bed. No one, it seemed, had an appetite left for eating.

Elizabeth stared at the woman and tried to fathom the news that bounced within her head but in no wise penetrated the recesses of her brain.

"Come, Elizabeth, sit down beside me," Lady Chesterton said softly. "It seems we are alone, again, we two."

Elizabeth sat, simply because the lady's words told her to do so. She had no power of her own to concentrate or act rationally. She seemed as a character moving about in a story, except that there was no book and the drama was very real.

"Strange—," Lady Chesterton said, "I recall the first time I saw you at Giltham Hall. I had to turn my head away, because you reminded me of the little infant I thought was drowned."

Elizabeth could do nothing but stare at the woman who was her real mother. *What will mother and father say,* she wondered.

"There is something else I must tell you, my dear," she said. "Your father left some money for you—a thousand pounds to be exact. It is yours."

"Mine?" Elizabeth whispered.

"Yes. It has remained sealed all these years. I thought I'd have to leave it there untouched. It's not much, but it will give you a small sense of independence."

"This is so hard to grasp," the girl said at last.

"It's a shock to all of us, Elizabeth." Lady Chesterton laid a cold hand on the girl's soft warm one. "You have no idea how glad I am to know you are alive and well. I am proud to claim you as my daughter."

"My lady, who—"

"Can you try to call me mother, Elizabeth? Please."

"Yes, I will try." Elizabeth felt the warmth of love coming from the woman's large brown eyes. Before she knew what really transpired, the woman gathered her in her arms and kissed her.

When they rose and walked toward the dining room, Elizabeth thought of Lord Giltham and the inheritance and her return to the house. She wondered about something else before she spoke the words. "Please, mother, I must know one more thing."

"I know what you are going to ask." The woman's eyes were sad once more.

"Who is my father?"

Lady Chesterton sighed deeply. "I have told no one except the doctor who delivered you, and he has kept my secret faithfully over the years. You have a right to know. But I feel I am betraying the man, for I loved him."

"Why didn't you marry him?"

"He was already married—with two sons. I was a widow with two children of my own. He didn't mean to hurt me, but we loved each other so deeply."

"Would I have known him?"

"No. He died later."

Elizabeth waited for her answer, but the lady struggled with the telling of it. For some time they walked the length of the passage and back. Lady Chesterton would touch her arm or her hair or just glance fondly her way.

At last the woman faced her daughter and whispered, "It was the elder Lord Shaftsbury."

The words struck Elizabeth's heart like a wound, deep and painful and sickening. The thought that Elias and she had the same father was a revulsion that seemed beyond bearing.

The lady saw the pain in Elizabeth's eyes. "Elias was nothing like your father, be assured. He was a handsome man—gentle, soft spoken, and kind. Elias had his mother's ways but not her looks. Even his mother was not as ugly as he was." She sighed again. "Poor William loves you so. Please stay and help him."

"For a few days, but then I must return to tell the parents I have known all these years." She didn't mention Lord Giltham, but she thought of him, too.

"Try to eat if you can," Lady Chesterton urged. "I must find my husband for this has been a blow to him, too." She squeezed the girl's hand and left her.

Elizabeth was too stunned to evince much of an appetite, but she did manage to take a piece of fruit and a little sweet tea. As she sat at the dining room table she stared at the marvelous appointments of the room—the high plastered ceiling, the handsome framed landscapes, and elegantly carved chairs. *All of this,* she thought, *is my mother's.*

Slowly Elizabeth rose, chose some fruit, a bit of meat and tea to put on a tray, and made her way to William's room. The door was closed, so she knocked lightly and waited for a response from within. None came. Again she knocked and waited until the soldier called flatly, "Come in."

Elizabeth approached the bed and placed the tray on a small table. "Please try to eat a little."

William turned his drawn face toward the girl and studied her carefully. "I loved you so."

"Loved, William? You love me no longer. A sister isn't someone to love?" She sat on the edge of the bed and stared into his eyes. "I'm pleased to have a brother for the first time in my life."

"We almost married, you and I—save for that foolish little bit of velvet about your neck." He put his hand on hers and sighed bitterly. "Somehow I felt all along that something would stand between us."

He reached over and pulled the girl to his breast, kissed her hair, and held her close. "My almost bride," he whispered.

"Yes, almost," she whispered in return. Then she pulled away and offered him the food. "Please, William, will you try to eat now?"

"You act like a provoking sister already."

"How would you know when you've never had one before?"

"Oh, I've heard talk." And he smiled.

Chapter 14

The days that followed were filled with walks and much talking about the war, relatives, and London. But Elizabeth could not seem to persuade either William or her mother that she must return to Giltham. Still she knew she must. She longed to see Jonathan, and she felt an obligation to care for Lady Giltham until she could find someone else.

Whether Lord Chesterton had forgiven his wife or not wasn't certain, for he kept occupied—rode a great amount in the park and read in the library.

Then one day Elizabeth watched the lord's valet make numerous trips to the front passage with various sized boxes.

"Is your father going away, William?" asked Elizabeth.

"Fishing. In Scotland. He always goes there in the summer after Parliament ends, and then mother and I follow in a few days. We let him have the freedom of some time without us."

"He goes alone?"

"No, Jonathan and some of the men will meet him there. Jonathan left Giltham Hall yesterday, I understand."

Elizabeth was stunned. "Are you quite certain Lord Giltham left already?"

"Yes."

Elizabeth feared the answer to her next question. "Will they stay all summer?"

"I can't say. They come and go as they want. But Jonathan said something about going on to the continent from there."

Elizabeth turned from William so he would not see the tears in her eyes. *Why did I let them talk me into staying?* she asked herself desperately. The only thing that was worse than the thought of life at Giltham Hall with Lady Giltham as her only companion was the prospect of service to some future wife of Jonathan's.

"Are you well, Elizabeth? You look positively shaken."

"Yes, I'm all right. But everything that has happened is so overwhelming to me."

"It is to both of us," he whispered.

Once William was recovered enough to travel, he and Lady Chesterton prepared for the journey to the summer lodge in Scotland.

"You should come with us," the lady told Elizabeth. "I would rather you didn't work. Heaven knows you have done enough of it."

"No. I could not do that for I promised to serve Lady Giltham for a year. I'll return to Giltham Hall until she can find a replacement," Elizabeth replied with finality.

"If you must. But we'll take you there and proceed on to Scotland." Lady Chesterton put her arm about her daughter and said softly, "I will write often and keep in touch with you. In time my husband will come to accept you as a daughter." She kissed her affectionately as if she couldn't shower enough attention on the girl.

The sun shone warm and bright between patches of darkening clouds the day they left Chesterton Manor. Here and there a thrush winged past and sought footing in a hedge, those hated new enclosures about Dumford that offered solace and safety to the birds but repelled some humans.

The carriage bounced over the rutted turnpike road and approached the main road running through the village of Giltham.

"You're very quiet, Elizabeth," said Lady Chesterton.

"Yes. I suppose I am. I must consider how to tell my parents all that has happened."

"May I meet them, Elizabeth? I would like to thank them personally." Lady Chesterton thought of the carpenter who came to her with the strip of cloth, and she pictured him with her little girl and the love he must have showered on Elizabeth.

"Yes, it would be good for you to meet them. Their cottage is the first one on the left as we turn onto the main road of Giltham."

When the carriage drew to a halt in front of the cottage, Lady Chesterton placed her hand on Elizabeth's. "You will want to go in alone," she said softly. "William and I will wait until you come for us."

Elizabeth nodded. It would be better that way, certainly. But either way it would not be easy.

Martha was cutting cabbage when the girl knocked lightly and entered the room. For an instant Elizabeth studied her before she threw her arms about the woman's neck and held her tightly. How could she say that she no longer belonged to her or this cottage?

It was a moment before she could trust her voice to say anything at all. Then she whispered, "I need to talk to you and father."

"He's in the shop. I'll ask him to come in."

The two sat down and faced their daughter, fully expecting to hear the announcement of her pending marriage.

Elizabeth hesitated a moment before she placed her hands on theirs. "I love you both more than I can say. Because of you I have found purpose for my life and faith in Christ."

She squeezed their hands a little tighter and the tears came. "This week I found something else, also. I wore the jewel you gave me. Because of it I found my real mother—and a half brother, too."

Matthew and Martha were too stunned to move.

"How can it be?" Martha whispered.

"I'd like them to be here when I explain that to you, mama. They are in the carriage waiting—"

"They're here? Now?"

"Yes," Elizabeth whispered tenderly.

"Oh, Matthew, I don't know if—. Are you leaving for good, Elizabeth?" cried Martha.

"No," she answered softly. "I'll remain at Giltham Hall as before, and I will see you often now that Elias is gone."

The three of them sat there together for a while, preserving the last few moments of their life as it was before.

Then the carpenter placed a calloused hand around his wife's shoulder. "We knew this might happen some day, didn't we, Martha? . . . We've been fortunate to have her for so many years."

He turned to Elizabeth. "Ask your mother and brother to come in. We shall be pleased to meet them."

Elizabeth placed her arms around both of them. "I will always love you as much as ever." Then she turned and went to the carriage.

When Lady Chesterton and William appeared in the doorway, Matthew and Martha Bardwell gasped. "Lady Chesterton! Lady Chesterton's not your mother, is she, Elizabeth?"

"Yes, and William is my half-brother."

Quietly Elizabeth explained all that Lady Chesterton had

told her, all except the identity of her father. That was her mother's secret and could only be revealed when she felt it was right to do so.

"You don't know how happy I am to find my daughter after all these years." Lady Chesterton said when Elizabeth had finished. "I had never forgotten her—not for a day."

"I'm sure you hadn't, my lady," Martha Bardwell replied slowly. "But she has been our daughter for so long—"

"I understand," said Lady Eleanor. It's been a great shock to us all." Then she rose. "I owe you so much. I can never repay you."

"Just having her was all we could ever want," said Matthew. "She has been a great joy to us. Let's say the Lord loaned her to us for a while."

"And for a short time, at least, I shall see you frequently, Elizabeth," Matthew added. "Before Lord Giltham left, he asked me to be his new steward."

"Oh, father, I am so happy for you." Elizabeth hugged the sturdy carpenter. "What about the enclosures?"

"Stopped until Lord Giltham's return—whenever that may be."

"That is good news," cried Elizabeth.

"We must go, for Lady Giltham is expecting us for dinner," said Lady Chesterton rising. "Again, my deepest thanks to you both for the care you've given my daughter." She smiled and reached for each of their hands. "Good-bye for now. But we will meet again."

Elizabeth kissed the Bardwells and whispered good-bye. Then she left the cottage to return to Giltham Hall.

Lady Giltham was resting on her chaise under the supervision of Dr. Sloane when the three were announced. "So, the erring one has returned, I see, and on the arm of her husband?" She stared intently as a hawk at Elizabeth. "I gave you credit for having more sense."

"Enough, Adelaide," answered Lady Chesterton, gathering control of her rising anger. "You are speaking to my daughter—not a daughter-in-law." She glanced at Dr. Sloane. "Tell her, doctor. Elizabeth knows already."

The doctor studied the girl and then Lady Chesterton. "It's true, Adelaide. I did deliver a baby girl twenty years ago. When I first saw Elizabeth and heard how Matthew Bardwell found her, I suspected that she might be Lady Chesterton's daughter."

Lady Giltham stared at the younger woman and for once in her life was speechless. "What do you mean?"

"Just what I said. She is the daughter that I thought was drowned at two months of age, along with her nurse. . . . So she needn't work for you, Adelaide. She needn't work at all."

Lady Giltham stared at Eleanor Chesterton. "This whole thing sounds preposterous. There is more to it than that, I'm sure. You are not telling all."

"What matters to me is that she is my lost daughter. The proof is absolute." Then Lady Chesterton turned to Elizabeth. "You needn't stay, you know."

"If Lady Giltham needs me, I shall stay. But if she doesn't, I'll make other arrangements."

"Of course, you'll stay. Your year isn't ended until September. We have an agreement."

"Adelaide, you will be good to her, will you not? For I shall be deeply hurt if you are not."

"Hmph, of course I will. But every child needs discipline from time to time." She stared at William. "So, you are brother and sister."

"Yes, that is correct," William answered.

"Well, I am shocked."

"I supposed you would be. Now, Adelaide, won't you have your footman show William and me to our rooms. It's about time for dinner."

With that Lady Chesterton dismissed the subject and would not let Lady Giltham pry for more details at dinner that night—or make any unpleasant comments.

Before she left the next day, Lady Chesterton drew Elizabeth aside and placed her arm about the girl's waist. "Adelaide has a sharp tongue, and if she mistreats you in any way please leave the premises. There are a few servants at Chesterton Manor, and you can go there to live anytime you care to."

"I will be all right. Really. I am used to the woman's ways." Elizabeth gave her mother a reassuring hug, and then Lady Chesterton joined her son in the waiting carriage. Elizabeth watched the coach rumble away until it was completely lost from view.

The days passed, and Elizabeth's faith was the sole sustaining force that kept her spirits from sinking, for she no longer had either William or Jonathan. Existing in the very place that Jonathan had quitted just weeks before brought back painful memories.

Oh, why doesn't Lady Giltham get a replacement for me, she wondered. *The two she interviewed yesterday seemed so right, but the woman rejected them as she would an old dress.*

Slowly the last days of June melted into the warm, sluggish days of July. Elizabeth took Lady Giltham for short walks onto the carriage sweep and for a few short ramblings into the garden where the flowers bloomed in full glory. But the lady only lent curses to the winds for her ailments rather than thanksgiving for all she possessed.

After safely returning to the hearth on these days, Lady Giltham would demand to be read or sung to—whatever was her whim of the hour. Elizabeth wept for the woman's stubborn will—the shield she had built against God and those around her.

Elizabeth felt caught by her new circumstances. To go to

the Bardwells would be awkward now, because of her altered position and the presence of a real mother, who might regard such a move as nonacceptance. And Chesterton Manor. How could she flee to its walls for protection when the master, himself, resented her presence there.

One morning in mid-July Lady Giltham awoke early with a pain in her arm. Not the usual dull annoyance, but a pain that seized and restricted her breathing.

Elizabeth heard the call and ran in to the woman's room. "What is it, my lady?"

"Get the doctor from Dumford—quickly," she whispered. "For I can't breathe."

The girl threw a robe about her and ran toward the servants' entrance to awaken the new butler. The sun had sent its first orange rays across the sky to faintly illumine the way without a candle. When she barged into his chamber and shook him awake, he cried out, "What do you want?"

"The lady's ill and must have a doctor immediately. Someone must go to Dumford and fetch him as soon as possible."

By the time Elizabeth returned to Lady Giltham's room, the woman was breathing with difficulty and held onto the girl's arm as a drowning man grasps at a rope thrown for rescue.

Elizabeth's foremost concern was the woman's soul, for she was facing eternity—staring it full in the face. "Can you hear me?" asked Elizabeth.

"Yes," she whispered.

"Is your heart right with God? Have you asked him to forgive you?"

The woman didn't answer, but closed her eyes, and for a horrible instant Elizabeth thought she was gone. The pain was intense, but she must get through to the woman. Five minutes might be too late.

"He wants to give you peace," she cried softly. "Just

breathe a prayer from your heart."

After an eternal length of time, Lady Giltham opened her eyes and stared into the girl's face. Tears squeezed out the corners of the lady's eyes and found their way in little rivulets down the creased lines of her skin. She smiled. Elizabeth knew all was as it should be, for the woman gave her hand a slight squeeze.

Elizabeth stayed with Lady Giltham until the doctor arrived to examine her. When he finished, the doctor talked to Elizabeth quietly in the passage. "She's had a severe heart seizure, and I doubt she will live. The lady is certainly placid enough and seems in good spirits, but I cannot guarantee that another won't follow. I'll stay here for the remainder of the day. . . . You look as if you could use a walk in the air."

"Yes, I think I could. I'll not be gone long." Then Elizabeth turned. "Shall we send word to her son in Scotland?"

"Yes. He ought to come immediately." The doctor nodded and went back to his patient.

Elizabeth walked out the side door and into the garden. Drops of rain hung on the roses and ivy and clung to the hedges. Elizabeth continued to walk about the garden paths and stare beyond the lofty oaks into the sky.

The wind whipped at her skirt and blew her hair across her face, but she was somehow numb to all of it until the approaching sounds of a horse drew her attention toward the house and carriage sweep. She was too far to see who the rider might be, so she continued to wander about the narrow pebbled avenues and shrubs. The half-open beauty of a rose caught her attention for an instant. As she turned to look at it she saw someone standing at the garden entrance.

She stopped and stared. Her breath caught in her throat. *Can it be?* she thought. *Is it–?* As she stared, unbelieving,

Jonathan rushed toward her, and she toward him. Their arms clasped one another with a lasting pledge.

"Elizabeth, my darling, oh, my darling," he whispered over and over again in his joy.

ONE MOMENT PLEASE...

...while you're sitting in the glow of this book's ending, isn't this the perfect time to make sure you won't miss a single book in our ALL NEW Chime series? Simply fill out the coupon below and mail with your payment TODAY...or look for them in your favorite bookstore.

ROMANCE AT REDHAVEN

by Kathleen Yapp

Traveling to the majesties of California Redwood territory, little did Jennifer realize the impact her presence would have on rugged, worldly David Cameron's world. Travel with her as she chronicles the lives in the Cameron Dynasty...and changes them...forever.

#52928.. **$ 2.50**

DEATH ON AN ISLAND

by Gayle C. Roper

Murder stalks the peaceful vacation retreat of Susannah Adams and Megan Simmons on a quiet Canadian Island. Who—out of a handful of vacationers—would have done it? And why? Will they make it out alive? And at what cost?

#52944.. **$ 2.50**

YES! I want to order the following Chime books!

☐ Romance at Redhaven .... **#52928, $ 2.50**
(plus .35 shipping & handling)

☐ Death on an Island .... **#52944, $ 2.50**
(plus .35 shipping & handling)

Illinois & California residents, add applicable sales tax:

TOTAL________________

Enclosed, please find my.....

☐ **check** ☐ **money order** ☐ **Visa** ☐ **MasterCard**

credit card no.____________________

SEND TO:

Name ____________________________

Address____________________________
(Box or Apt. No.)

City____________State____________Zip ________

ORDER FROM:

JENNY VAN TREESE, David C. Cook Publishing Co.
850 N. Grove Ave., Elgin, IL 60120